# CALLOUS CRIMINAL

## VICIOUS VIPERS MC 3

LYNN BURKE

# CALLOUS CRIMINAL

I'm a cold hearted criminal, and I've lived a callous life as the Sergeant at Arms of the Vicious Vipers MC. I spent most of my childhood as a victim, and because of the junkie who raised me, I hate to be touched.

But her...

The social worker my fingers itch to reach for—she's wholesome. Kind. Too good for a man like me, and yet, I can't curb my weakness to be near her.

When one of her teenage clients needs protection from the same type of man who hurt my sister, I know I'll be revealing my true self, my darker side, to help the girl.

For her.

I'll lose the only person I've found who values my feelings above her own—the woman whose sweet nature is a force to be reckoned with.

I know I should walk away, but how do I leave the heart I didn't know I still had behind?

# DEDICATION

*For Amber & Pia*

# CONTENTS

## RYKER

A group of teenagers huddled together, waiting for their fancy as fuck coffees, laughing over top of the whirl of the milk frothing thing behind the counter. The murmurs from the long line at the register and those at the tables around me created a buzz beneath their carrying on.

I'd been sitting for over an hour with the ongoing noise, waiting and hoping he would show his ugly mug. I knew he was in town, and he had to have heard I'd been asking around about him.

I'd also made it known I sat at Dunks every morning the previous week drinking coffee like a fiend.

I inhaled the scent of coffee and toasting bagels, but couldn't stomach the thought of eating so early in the morning. At least I'd managed to escape the sweltering heat outside while riding my Harley to Dunks.

Summer in Southie—a time of freedom for the young, a time to kick back and relax, maybe make a buck or two. I'd only done the third when I'd been a young punk like the noisy, too-happy fuckers on the other side of Dunks. Running messages and delivering drugs for the Irish mafia along with my two best friends Klingon and Martínez had lined my pockets and had given me a thirst for danger and violence.

We'd been inseparable, three peas in a pod, one Irish, one black, and one Latino. Opposites in every way except shared enjoyment of being a hoodlum and making money. My issues with physical touch hindered me from getting the pussy they had, but I'd had a girl or two in my back pocket who didn't mind sucking me off with their hands behind their back at my request.

A mouth on my dick, I could handle. Fingertips and palms other than my own, I could not—no matter how much I longed for it.

Gaze flitting around the coffee shop and trying to ignore the heart-eyed couple beside me with their fingers clasped atop the table, I considered my week away from the Vipers' club.

I'd been poking around and listening, searching for answers about the cartel we'd beheaded a few months earlier. Heading south had been my idea, though. I'd needed to get the fuck out of the club, away from the love birds and public displays of affection from my two brothers who'd supposedly found their soul mates.

Who the fuck was I kidding?

Seeing Warden and Stone with their women made it obvious that sort of shit *did* exist. Both were pussy whipped. Madly in love. Sickeningly so, touching non-fucking stop, and rousing a covetousness inside me I never knew existed even as a young kid whose best friends got all the action.

I scowled at the couple beside me as she laughed and he lifted her hand to his lips.

Fucking sick of it.

Couldn't fucking escape cupid's work and knowing I would never experience that sort of emotion or affection only pissed me off more.

At least I drank less whiskey away from the club. With the path I'd been on, I'd end up like my bastard father—but my luck, probably taking lives along with mine for driving under the influence. I'd turned to black coffee and ended up jittery as fuck from sucking it down like water in liquor's place.

I lifted the third cup of coffee I'd gotten since arriving at Dunks, scowling deeper to find it lukewarm on my tongue. Another hour of my life fucking wasted?

A shiny Mercedes pulled into the parking lot, tinted windows giving me the first shot of adrenaline and hope I'd felt in a long fucking time. I leaned forward to keep the car in sight through the big glass window on my right.

Once parked on the far side of the lot, the driver stepped out and opened the back door.

The fucker showed.

I sipped my cool coffee, gaze tracking him through the window as he adjusted his shades and straightened his suit coat.

Fucking suit in Southie in the middle of a goddamn heat wave. The fuck was wrong with him? As a kid, he'd always been vain as fuck, needing his hair gelled and slicked back, clothes unwrinkled, and new converse every other week.

He stepped inside, head swiveling right to left before stalling out on my hunched form. A flick of his hand removed his sun glasses, his dark eyes pinned on me as he moved my way. His hair slicked back as usual, but at least he hadn't covered the gray hair shooting backward above his temples.

I'd just shaved mine the fuck off when it started to thin out up top in my early twenties. With a shaved head and full beard, I felt it made me look mean as fuck—the look I'd decided on after taking up with the Vipers. Mean and untouchable.

"Heard you were looking for me." Martínez settled across from me.

"Visiting with my mom for a few weeks," I stated a different truth. "Figured I'd see what you were up to. Been awhile."

"I heard she wasn't doing well."

I nodded, and he studied me, his eyes as dead as a week-old corpse—and just as cold.

"Looks like you've done well for yourself," I said with a wave toward the fancy as fuck car and the driver who'd stayed outside to light up a cigarette. "Fucking chauffeur, and is that an Italian suit? Silk, I'm guessing."

Martínez glanced over my old white t-shirt with its stretched out neck and black leather cut worn soft from years of abuse. "And it looks like you're still running the Vipers' chop shop."

"Don't know what you're talking about." Deadpan, I kept my focus on his face, wishing I had a cocky grin leftover from our childhood days.

"Lying fuck." Martínez's eyes lightened a bit, and he chuckled. "Everyone knows what you and your *so-called* brothers do. Greased pockets is all that stands between you crooked fucks and jail time."

So-called.

They weren't blood, but my Viper brothers knew what loyalty meant, something Martínez had lost touch with over the years.

I shrugged like I didn't give a shit about his opinion and sipped, waiting to see what he'd give up.

Martínez continued to study me, and I kept my mouth shut, knowing he'd start talking and give me what I wanted. Fucker couldn't keep from talking—bragging—when he'd been a punk-ass teen. Bad habits lingered on that sorry fuck like stench on a pile of hot shit.

The loud teenagers finally walked outside, but the whirling of bean grinders and frothing continued for the unending line of customers as we sat in silence.

"You know what happened to my cousin?" Martínez finally broke our standoff.

I dipped my head once with a slight nod. "Heard Arturo disappeared awhile back."

"He's dead."

The back of my scalp prickled, but I didn't let a tic of emotion show on my face. I'd seen the knife stab into him twice. Watched him bleed out from the slice across his neck. It had given me a shit ton of satisfaction, even though I hadn't been the one holding the blade. "You sure?"

"He wouldn't have left his empire willingly."

"Well, that's a shame. Sorry for your loss." The lie came easy. The fucker had deserved to die—and I'd enjoyed watching Stone end his waste-of-sperm existence.

"Remember that time Klingon and you duped me into believing Mrs. Jenson was hot for my dick?"

I huffed a laugh even though Martínez's face stayed passive as fuck rather than light up with teenage memories. "Horney fuck—your dick led the way to her place."

"And her husband kicked the shit out of me."

I tipped my head back and forth a few times as though recalling the memory. "Pretty sure that fight earned you that badass rep you enjoyed having."

"Breaking a cop's face is nothing compared to what I'll do if I find out you and the Vipers had anything to do with Arturo's death."

I stared at him, unblinking as my heart rate kicked up a gear.

As expected, Martínez opened his mouth as I sat in silence. "I know you've got your connections down here in Southie, but so do I," he said under his breath, leaning over the table, his dark eyes full of threat—and promise. "You want to know who's leading the cartel? It's me, Ryker, but I'm not the friend you grew up with all those years ago. Arturo took me into his inner circle when I left Boston. Unlike you and Klingon, he understood what family meant, what loyalty meant."

I barely held in my snort and sipped again, fighting off a grimace at the cold bitterness attempting to settle in my clenching gut.

"And," Martínez continued while standing and adjusting his silk suit coat, "I'm going to be just as loyal to his memory. His plans for the family business."

A few words of flippant good luck entered my brain, but I bit them back, merely holding my old friend's gaze. I silently dared him to spew more shit. More threats—even though I knew as leader of the Martínez cartel he sure as fuck had the means and connections to follow through.

Martínez eventually turned on his heel and

strode back out into the bright sun, but his threat hovered over me like a goddamn cloud, chilling me more than the AC blasting overhead. If the cartel came gunning for our club, it wouldn't just be bikers and club whores who would meet their end. If Martínez planned on being loyal to Arturo and his ways, even my brothers' kids and old ladies wouldn't escape his wrath.

The second the Mercedes disappeared into traffic, I pulled my cell from my back pocket.

"Ryker," Vigil answered after one ring. "Whatcha got?"

"Martínez took over, just like I figured," I muttered, finally sitting back in my chair even though my shoulders refused to relax.

"Fuck."

A shiver licked over my skin as I waited, half-hoping Vigil would tell me to take care of the problem before he *became* a problem.

"You talk to him?" Vigil said with a grunt.

"Just now."

"Where's he at?"

I knew Vigil wasn't asking about location, but his goddamn headspace. "Hell bent," I replied, keeping my voice to a murmur so the couple beside me wouldn't hear even if they were caught up in one another. "Made it clear he'll clean up that shit if he finds the mess."

"Fuck," Vigil muttered again. "Get your ass back to the club."

In my head, I compared Mom's shitty condo where I'd been crashing for a week to the love-shack club outside Topsfield for all of two seconds before shaking my head. "I'm gonna stick around down here for a little while longer," I told Vigil while standing and striding toward the exit. "Mom's not doing all that great, and my sister likes having me around to help."

My half-empty coffee cup thumped into the bottom of the trashcan at the same time Vigil offered condolences.

He knew my mom was on her way out—but he also knew I didn't give more than a single shit about the woman who hadn't done her job as a mother. She hadn't caused my hatred of being touched, but she hadn't done anything to protect me from the PTSD I'd ended up with, either.

"Come home when you're ready," Vigil said, and I shoved my cell back into my pocket while pushing open the door.

The sun hit my face along with hot, humid air stinking of exhaust, and I turned toward my bike.

Head down, focused on a cell, a woman hurried toward me, and I scuttled sideways to escape her fast clip.

Not fucking fast enough.

She slammed into my side and grasped hold of my bare forearm, a squeak of surprise ripping from her mouth as her cell clattered to the sidewalk.

"Oh! I'm so sorry!" She lessened her grip on my arm, and I clenched my teeth as my stomach knotted fast as fuck.

Not wanting to be a complete asshole, I didn't shake off her hold but waited for her to steady herself in her sandals. Her soft touch burned my skin. Sent a shot of need to lash out with my fists along with an energetic zap to my dick I hadn't felt in years.

I pulled away the second I could and bent to retrieve her cell while she righted her purse and the sweater she had draped over one arm.

Standing, I handed her the phone she'd dropped.

Straight blonde hair brushed her shoulders, her blue-green eyes and pale lashes unframed or painted by makeup. Pink flushed her cheeks, and she pressed her lips together, drawing my focus to the sparkling gloss coating them while reaching for her cell.

I made sure to keep our fingers from touching. "Not a problem," I stated with a gruffness I hadn't meant to do while noting the flush across her chest and the hint of cleavage peeking at the top of her plain, buttoned up blouse.

She smiled up at me, a plain-Jane yet classically beautiful woman who smelled like fresh, juicy watermelon.

My mouth watered, and I stepped back out of her way. With a dip of my head, I moved around her, intent on my bike—and escaping the weird vibe breaking me out into a sweat atop the bright as fuck sun.

*It* is *the heat*, I told myself while fighting the need to look over my shoulder. See if her back was as pretty as her front, even if she hadn't dressed to showcase the curves I'd caught a glimpse of.

The bike roared to life between my thighs, and I glanced toward Dunks while pulling on my helmet. She'd gone inside, escaping the heat, but I couldn't see her past the glare of the sun on the shop's windows.

Lips set in a line, I put on my shades and pulled out, already sweating through my t-shirt. I had to stop again for an old woman with her dolly of groceries in the cross walk a block up the road. She moved with more spring in her step than Mom even though they appeared about the same age, and seconds later, I shot down the road, my skin cooling in the wind whipping past me.

I grimaced at the thought of going back to Mom's with its single window-unit in the living room, but any place was better than the club with all its cupid bullshit. Deciding on the long route back to Mom's place, I held out my left arm signaling a turn.

Martínez's threat still hung over my head like the sun baking my back, but I trusted Klingon's ability to clean up the mess the Vipers had made while taking down the skin sale and handful of assholes out in Vegas earlier that spring.

The scent of watermelon overshadowed both, and I suddenly didn't trust myself or the confidence I'd banked on a mere fifteen minutes earlier.

## 2

## PIA

Arrestingly cold eyes...

I couldn't rid my mind of their green depths that chilled more than heated, and the black lashes framing them. And the equally hardened forearm that had flexed beneath my grasp...

Sighing, I moved ahead one spot in line, needing an iced coffee to soothe the dryness in my throat. I'd planned on a hot cup regardless of the heat outdoors, but the second I'd slammed into the tall biker in the parking lot, my innards lit on fire. Burned up to a crisp the second our gazes had connected.

I'd recognized the tension in him beneath my fingertips—the inability to withhold from flinching. He'd been hurt same as so many people I'd fought to help over the years. The teenagers I'd devoted my life to, the unwanted, those left to the system and whatever foster parents willing to take them in.

Once inside Dunks, I'd watched the biker drive off on his chopper, his black leathers and boots much too hot for summer, yet required, I'd supposed, for riding.

I moved another step closer to the counter, glancing over the array of fresh donuts, the icing and sprinkles enticing me to ignore the fact I didn't need another inch on my thighs.

The thought of the stranger between them, his bike rumbling beneath us, rekindled the fire he'd invoked, and I squeezed my legs together beneath my frumpy skirt as wetness dampened my granny panties.

Just as alluring as his virile masculinity, the sense of freedom his bike offered, tempted my imagination to run wild.

Wind whipping through my shoulder-length hair, the coolness kissing my heated face. Complete liberation from the window-less, tiny office awaiting me.

"Miss Pia!"

I stepped forward, pushing aside dreams of freedom and smiling at the young man behind the counter. "Jesse—it's been forever! How are you doing?"

"Great." He grinned. "Tell me you aren't going with your usual scalding coffee?"

I shook my head, glancing once more at the strawberry iced donuts behind him. "I'll take it over ice today."

"Sure thing, Miss Pia. Anything else?"

*One hot biker with cold, hazel-green eyes...*

"That'll be it today," I told him, ignoring the call of the sugary carbs and freedom I would never have to whet my appetite.

Jesse moved off to get my coffee, and I considered the barely eighteen-year-old I'd had beneath my wing for over eight years. He'd been one of the lucky ones, while in and out of foster homes, he hadn't been troubled by aggression or unwanted advances. He'd never found his forever home, but he'd had it easier than most.

So many of my kids struggled through their final years in foster care. One had disappeared a year earlier—Sophia Delgado—a beautiful Latina her final foster father had lusted after.

I hadn't been able to get her out of the home in time. At seventeen, she'd left me a message telling me what he'd attempted to do, and that she was done with the system.

She'd erased herself from the face of the earth as far as I and the law who didn't give two shits about a family-less runaway knew. No body had ever turned up, though. I hoped for the best rather than the probable truth of her existence as a sex slave in some far-off country.

"Here you are, Miss Pia." Jesse handed me my coffee in exchange for a five dollar bill.

"Do you remember Dasia?" I asked, watching his face closely as he made change.

A hint of a frown creased his forehead for a second. "The little redhead from the Carters?"

I nodded, accepting my change, my throat tightening over the latest disappearance. "Have you seen her around town at all?"

"No, ma'am. Is she in trouble?"

Expecting my smile would wobble, I tried for one anyway. "She left her foster parents' home four days ago and never returned."

Jesse's face fell, and I longed to lean over the counter and hug the sweet young man. "I hope you find her."

"If you see her…"

"I'll let you know, Miss Pia." He nodded. "Promise."

Two minutes later, I drove toward Boston, the windows rolled down rather than cranking the AC, enjoying the hot breeze blowing through my hair— as close to freedom as I expected I would ever get to experience.

Had Dasia run off for the same reasons as Sophia? She'd told me she hated the newest home she'd been placed in, but I'd begged her to hang in there with only a few months until she turned eighteen...

I exhaled a heavy breath and pulled into my Monday through Friday parking garage, escaping the sun, the darkness weighing like the layers of cement and steel overhead.

Both Sophia and Dasia were beautiful young woman, on the cusp of adulthood. Ready to begin their own lives, free to choose what they would. Had Dasia chosen to leave on her own as Sophia had, or had someone noted her natural ginger beauty and stolen her off the streets?

Cold shivers licked at my spine as I walked through the dark parking garage toward the exit leading back to Boston's downtown. Sweat trickled down my back and between my breasts but did little to cool my body.

The heavy scent of exhaust clogged my lungs, and even though the bright sunlight squinted my eyes once more, I breathed easier once outside the claustrophobic atmosphere of the garage.

My hole in the wall office didn't offer much better, but at least clean air filtered through the air conditioning ducts thanks to my boss who insisted on purifiers throughout the office space.

A few phone calls into my day provided no news on Dasia. My daily online search for Sophia and missing Latina girls provided the same as every morning. Sighing, I sipped the last of my ice-melted, watered-down coffee, and stared at the search bar on my computer screen.

Even though my door remained closed, murmurings from the neighboring offices droned through the thin walls. The AC kicked off, and with seconds, heat prickled my skin again.

I closed my eyes against the feeling of the walls creeping in on me, counting to ten and back down to keep anxiety from rising and tightening my throat.

Breathing steadily with purpose to stay calm, I opened my eyes and typed in Vicious Vipers without thought, remembering the rockers on the back of hazel-eye's leather vest.

News articles and images popped up.

Group photo...

I clicked on the picture from a charity event they'd been involved in a few years earlier, my gaze landing on the bearded man I'd plowed into that morning. Cold eyes, even in black and white... My heart jumped as I noted the names listed beneath.

Fingertip trailing air above my screen, I found him.

Ryker McGrath.

I focused on his face once more, seeing beyond the cool reflection I expected he masked himself with to hide the hurt within. Unable to help from digging, I opened another tab and searched his name, perusing articles and various websites.

A Southie boy who'd left for the North Shore twenty years earlier. Forty-three, single, and a mechanic. The Sergeant at Arms for the Vipers' local chapter.

I imagined being one of the bandana-wearing women on the back of the bikes—skin tight jeans even if they wouldn't flatter my figure, shit-kicker boots ... rooting out the cause of Ryker's pain and helping to heal the wounds deep inside him.

Shaking my head, I pushed thoughts of romance and breathing easy and free from my mind.

I needed to get a grip—I had work to do.

Reality sucked a big one.

Closing out all five browsers, I considered who else I might call, who else might have heard from or might have seen both of my missing girls. I prayed they still lived even though I felt *I* didn't while choosing to help the kids who needed me.

"Someone must know where they are." I picked up my phone and dialed another of the young adults I still kept in touch with since their release from the state's care.

*They're who I live for*, I reminded myself, but the truth I'd spent over ten years doing so didn't ease the new ache—the longing for *more*—inside my chest.

3
———

**RYKER**

The window unit in Mom's condo ran on high, but it didn't do much to lessen the stifling heat in the small place. I swore in my head while shutting the door behind me, disappointed to not find it a bit cooler inside than out or the fact the stale cigarette stench from Mom's bad habit still clung to the walls.

My sister Jenny sat at the kitchen table, her face drawn and pale, a mug in front of her.

I glanced back at the hallway leading to the two bedrooms. "How's she doing?"

Jenny shrugged and let out a heavy exhale. "Back to muttering about our shit head father and what a great man he was."

My lip curled as I pulled the coffee pot out to

pour myself a mug. "Want more?" I asked, gesturing to Jenny's mug.

"Sure."

I filled her mug, put the pot back, and settled into the rickety chair across the table from her.

"Hospice nurse just left," Jenny said as I sipped, her hands wrapping around her mug as though to warm them.

Scalding, fucking delicious, coffee slid down to my stomach that had yet to recover from the incident at Dunks—Martínez and that damn fine Jane Doe's fingertips.

"Got any watermelon in the fridge?" I heard myself ask.

Jenny frowned at me. "What?"

"Never mind." I sipped again, fighting off a frown at the lingering tingle in my forearm, and glanced around the condo I'd been paying for since Mom had gotten sick. For over a year, I'd single-handedly supported her and Jenny, from rent to cell phones, groceries and cable. Came easy since I'd paid off my own house up in Topsfield years earlier. The Vipers' chop shop did well—and I oversaw the daily operations except while on vacation. As though I took them often...

"When are you heading home?"

I shrugged and met Jenny's inquisitive stare. More green than mine, her hazel eyes peered at me as though reading through clear to my soul. Younger by almost five years, single due to her disinterest in dicks since one had been shoved inside her against her will while a twenty-something innocent.

That fucker had met his end earlier in the year, compliments of me and my knife. Looking into his eyes while slicing his neck and watching blood pour down over his front had been one of the better moments of my life—if only it had given me the satisfaction I'd hoped for.

I'd told her about the fucker's death, but that truth hadn't helped her move on, either. Celibate to the extreme, Jenny didn't even bother with dating. Mom's illness had given her something to focus on after years of battling depression and psych ward stays, but I feared what she would do after Mom finally gave up the ghost.

"You shouldn't be here, Ryk."

I met Jenny's stare.

"You ought to find yourself a good woman and never come back. This place is nothing but a life suck. It's pulled you down even in the week you've been here."

I rubbed at my forearm, the desire for watermelon hitting me again. "Not gonna happen," I muttered, ripping my hand away and wishing for something ten times stronger than black coffee.

Jenny eyed my forearm before turning her focus on my face again. "Still?"

"Always."

Lips pursed, she finally looked away, her tired eyes gazing out the window overlooking the apartment building across the road. A lone car horn muffled through.

"It wasn't," I said before she could spout off the shit she always did when our father's memory entered conversation and she blamed herself for what he'd done to me.

"Thank you," she whispered, turning toward me once more, tears in her eyes.

"I'd do it a thousand times over to protect you, Jenny. I just wish I could have been here every time he came home drunk." Guilt ate at my gut like it always did when I thought of my later teenage years and how Jenny had inherited his wrath in my absence. Wasn't her fault, no matter what she'd claimed over the years. I'd always taken the punishment, turned his anger toward me whenever she'd gotten into trouble.

It hadn't always been like that, though. Our

father hadn't started ignoring me and my need for affection until Jenny had been born—but I'd never told her that, nor would I ever. Mom had serious post-partum, and her depression pushed our father toward drugs and alcohol. But, it'd been his decision to take a turn down that slippery slope—not Jenny's fault.

"That fucker is dead, too," I told her, wishing I'd been the one to spill his blood. It'd been a drunken car accident, and thankfully he'd only taken his own life. It's what had started Mom on *her* downward spiral of drugs and alcohol. Her body finally had enough. It was just a matter of time.

Death hung like a shroud, black and heavy, over the condo, and like Jenny had said, I felt it pulling me under, lining beneath my eyes as it had done to her. She'd always appeared defeated in stance and self-confidence since *that day*, though.

"When Mom passes, you're moving up north with me."

Jenny jerked her head toward me at the declaration.

"You need to get outta Southie," I expanded on what I hadn't planned on offering, but with it being out... "Fucking change of scenery will do you good and I've got two extra bedrooms going to waste at my house."

Jenny let out a heavy exhale again, her eyes lighting up the slightest bit. "And what happens when some lady comes along, steals your heart, and gets all fat and hormonal with your brats?"

"Not gonna happen," I grumbled.

She snorted a fake as fuck laugh. "I just might take you up on that. Hell. Maybe what I need is a badass biker to get me over my dick aversion."

"Fuck." I scowled. "Don't even talk like that. One of my brothers so much as looks at you sideways, I'll break his goddamn nose."

"I always found crooked noses sexy."

"Shit." I eyed my sister, knowing she joked by the saucy tilt to one corner of her mouth—yet almost wishing one of my brothers would help to heal her, set her free. "You take an interest in one, you tell me first, yeah?"

"Yeah."

We sat in silence for a little, the most comfortable I'd been in a long ass time.

"Actually, I was thinking that I might go to Vegas for a couple weeks to visit Phoebe once Mom passes. *Really* get the hell out of here for a while."

I nodded, thinking that was just as good as her

moving up north with me right away. "That works, too. How's she been?"

Phoebe, Jenny's best friend from childhood, had headed west while still in high school and her dad had taken a big-wig job at some casino. They'd called each other PB&J when kids, and had been close ever since even though thousands of miles separated them.

"Doing good. Works at the same casino as her dad. Waitressing." Jenny shrugged. "Says she loves it."

"It'd be one hell of a change of scenery," I said, remembering the dry heat and desert I'd traipsed through earlier in the spring to help rescue Stone's woman.

Jenny let out another heavy sigh and glanced back down the hallway again. "Well, Mom isn't going to need me much longer. What's the point of sticking around here? I'd only end up cramping your style eventually—"

"You make better coffee than I do."

She let out a small, real laugh, something I hadn't heard pass her lips in years. "You and your coffee."

"I think it's a good idea, Jenny," I said, my lips even twitching at her lingering, rare smile. "Take off.

Get the hell out of here and see the world. Mom doesn't have much, but that life insurance policy I took out on her a few years back will give you enough to just live and not worry about responsibilities for a while. Fuck knows, you deserve it."

Tears filled her eyes. "Thanks, Ryk. I love you, you know that, right?" Her whisper warmed my heart, something I hadn't felt for a long fucking time. I scratched at my chest.

"Yeah," I said, my voice gruff, but rather than say it back, I decided to respond to her original question about how long I planned on staying in Southie. "I'll hang out until the end."

Jenny nodded, peering into her coffee mug. "Only be a couple days, the nurse said."

I didn't give two shits. "I've got my lawyer putting everything in order. This place will be yours until you decide what you're going to do. Here, Vegas, or my place. You do whatever the fuck you want."

"Thanks, Ryk."

I eyed her fingers still wrapped around her mug, wishing I could squeeze them and tell her I loved her back.

Instead, I dipped my head and got up. "Got some calls to make, then I'm heading out for the night."

"You're the best, Ryk."

Her whisper followed me back the hallway, but I pretended to not hear.

———

I sat in a dark corner of the seedy strip joint a few blocks from Mom's, nursing a beer, my attention on the spot-lit stage, but my focus beyond the redhead and her perky tits.

The younger woman was more my brother Devil's type than mine, anyway, with her sultry looks and sexy moves. Sassy flashes of her blue eyes didn't do jack shit for me like it seemed the men sitting around the stage tucking singles into her thong.

The bright red of her hair, however, reminded me of the scent of watermelon tormenting me all damn day. I'd even stopped by a grocery store to get some pre-cut shit in a container. While sweet and cold, the fruit hadn't quenched my thirst.

My forearm tingled, and scowling, I sipped at my drink while wishing it'd been a shot of whiskey sliding down my throat. I'd thought I could pick up a woman to suck me off—if she didn't mind getting on her knees in some alleyway and not touching me with anything other than her mouth. The joint I sat in hadn't let me down in the past whenever I'd hit Southie for a day or two, but I wasn't feeling it.

The wholesome Jane Doe from earlier in the day haunted my goddamn mind, and the thought of some whore in a back alley didn't so much as twitch my dick. *Fucking waste of time,* I muttered inside my head, trying like fuck to focus on the youngster on stage.

Too young, but perky as fuck and built for sin. Flaming red hair, curves in all the right places, an ass made for plundering, and eyes flashing with the type of sass a couple of my brothers wouldn't mind taming.

My dick still didn't twitch, and I huffed with annoyance.

*Fucking waste of time.*

## 4

## PIA

Heat flooded my cheeks as I studied the front of the establishment I had every intention of entering. I stalled, though, eyeing the poorly lit parking lot from where I'd parked across the street to watch the club's entrance.

I'd gotten the call I'd been waiting for—but on my cell, and hours after I'd left the office.

Jessie, the sweetheart, had asked around town and gotten a lead into my latest missing girl case. The news wasn't what I had hoped to hear, but better than a kidnapping and sex slave outcome.

Letting out a slow exhale, I grabbed my purse off the passenger seat of my old Chevy, and climbed out into the sweltering night. Sweat instantly sprang across my forehead and chest, and I cursed the size of my breasts for the millionth time since they'd sprouted when I'd turned ten.

I held my chin high while striding across the street in my sandals. I'd opted for my tightest jeans —daydreaming about being that biker chic fantasy I'd been having all day—but I'd gone with my usual frumpy shirt to hide my upper curves. God knew they drew enough attention without my highlighting them.

I pulled open the door, a blast of cold air sweeping over me along with muffled thumps beyond the foyer I found myself in. The dimly lit entrance stank of stale smoke and sweat.

A guy in all black sat on a stool beside the main entrance, and his once-over down my body heated my face as the door clanked shut behind me.

"Hey, darlin'."

My smile wobbled as I eyed the door he hovered near. "Can I go in?"

His gaze slid down over me again as he stood. "Go right ahead."

He used a big paw to push in the inner door, and the scent of booze and aftershave slammed into me along with the bass of a song. I slipped inside, blinking at the darkness—and the spotlight on the stage searing my retinas until my eyes adjusted.

*Dasia.*

"Oh, thank God." I shouldn't have stared at her bared body, but couldn't help myself. Gorgeous and perfect ... even if I didn't like women in a sexual way. She moved with fluid grace while dancing, and I fought the green monster inside who loved to torment my self-confidence.

I moved closer, purse clutched in front of me, as awareness of my surroundings settled over me. Darkness in every corner, lust hanging in the air and tingling my skin—danger for Dasia, I felt sure, even if she had been of age.

A cool ripple of unease skittered down my spine, raising the hairs on my neck as I stepped beneath a soft overhead light. The left side of my face burned like I'd stayed too long beside a fire.

Dasia turned toward me while dancing, blinking as our eyes met. She hesitated for less than a heartbeat before continuing with her gyrations, although a bit less sure of herself. I shifted on my sweating feet while waiting, choosing to watch her rather than take in the men salivating over her tight, young body. I didn't even have the gall to sneak a peek to my left and find out why that side of my face continued to burn.

The song ended—not nearly soon enough—and

she grabbed her discarded top from the stage, yanking it into place, her gaze returning to me. She hopped off stage as patrons continued to hoot and holler, their grabby hands missing flesh as she scooted across the strip club toward me.

"Dasia." I managed to keep my lips from pressing into a thin line of disproval ... barely.

"Miss Pia," she rushed to say, glancing around us as she drew close enough to talk over the next song taking over the speakers. She grasped my arm and drew me back the way I'd come in, close to the door. "Please don't say anything."

My heart broke as she peered up at me, tears welling in her heavily-made up eyes. Sparkles brightened her eyelids, and a sheen of sweat covered the rest of her face.

"I can't let you do this, Dasia," I said, needing to almost holler in order for her to hear me.

She spun to take off, but I grabbed hold of her arm. "Please," she mouthed, a tear sliding down her cheek as I drew her close once more.

"I have to take you back. Give me a few days, Dasia—I promise I'll get you placed elsewhere."

"I can't go back there at all!"

"What did he do?"

Her lip trembled, and the hurt in her eyes knifed me in the chest, stealing my breath.

"What's going on?"

Another man in all black approached, and Dasia straightened, flashing a fake smile his way.

"Pia, this is my boss, Mikey," Dasia hollered.

I loosened my hold on Dasia's arm, but didn't let her go. "She's seventeen," I blurted with a frown. "And a ward of the state."

Mikey jerked his heard toward Dasia, a scowl denting his brow. "You lied?"

Dasia kept her lips pressed tight.

"You're fired. Get out."

Another tear slipped free as Dasia nodded. "C-can I go get my stuff?" I barely heard her question over the blasting music.

A muscle ticked in Mikey's jaw. "I'll take you back there myself." He glanced over at me, giving me a once-over as his bouncer had done. "I didn't know. You, stay put," he ordered, putting his face close to my ear. "I'll have her back here in two minutes with all her shit."

I considered insisting I go along—but Mikey didn't grab her in anger, merely motioned her toward another door with his head. He stalked after her, but he seemed more upset she'd lied than intent on hurting her in any way.

Another shiver slid down over me. Once Dasia and Mikey disappeared through the "Employees Only" door, I gave in and turned toward the dark corner opposite the bar on my left as though drawn by a cat to catnip. Cold eyes peered at me—and lit me on fire from the inside out in one rushed heartbeat.

Ryker McGrath.

I gulped as he stood, his gaze unwavering from my heating face. Temptation to stay in place warred with an instinct to flee.

I didn't move other than my heart thumping harder. Faster. Outmatching the bass overhead.

He held my stare rather than check me out like the other two men had done, even though interest definitely sparked between us.

"You alright?" he asked loudly, leaning close enough I could fill my lungs with the fresh scent of whatever soap he used.

I nodded, my pulse thrumming throughout my entire body. "Yes." My smile faltered as I clutched my purse tighter. "Just here to pick up Dasia—she doesn't belong here."

Ryker's downward glance stalled out on my lips.

"No offence, little lamb, but you don't exactly look like you belong here either."

"I'm her social worker," I blurted, my voice high pitched and flaming me from chest to hair line.

He glanced at the door Mikey had led her through. "Underage?"

I nodded.

The beard lining his jaw twitched as though he'd clenched his teeth for a brief moment before turning back toward me. "Do you need any help?"

I opened my mouth to claim I had no clue, but the door to my right opened once more, and Dasia scuttled toward me in an oversized t-shirt and leggings, a duffle bag over her shoulder, and Mikey still on her heels. The scowl remained on his face.

A muscle in Mikey's jaw ticked as they approached. "If I'd known..."

I offered a smile. "We'll pretend like this never happened, won't we, Dasia?" I hollered.

She rolled her eyes, but moved along with me when I grasped her forearm to lead her out of that hell hole.

Into the hot night—Ryker followed along, I noted as the door shut behind us. The loss of thumping music eased the tension in my head I hadn't realized had taken up resident.

"Thank you for your offer," I said, turning to smile at him and releasing Dasia's arm.

He nodded, glancing over at Dasia. "You alright, kid?"

Lips in a thin line and her mascara a mess of tear tracks down her face, she nodded.

His focus returned to my eyes, and I froze beneath his stare. Deer in headlights. Moth to flame. All those cheesy metaphors hadn't ever meant a damn thing to me when it came to men, but in that moment, I understood them perfectly.

Ryker McGrath had snagged my attention, tunnel-visioning everything but him to the edge of my mind, ready to blink from existence. Yearning to step closer, sniff and lick like a damn animal, for crying out loud, itched my feet in their sandals. I wanted to smooth my thumb over the lines between his eyebrows, flutter my fingertips along his lips. Press my ear to his chest and drown in the thumping heartbeat beneath.

"I'll see ya around."

I blinked, reality rushing back with his muttered words, and I stared after him as he turned and strode away, shoulders rigid, footfalls leading him away from me, sure and steady.

"Miss Pia?"

I tore my focus off his retreating back and forced a smile, having forgotten all about the young woman in my care.

Dasia's lips quirked. "You've got it bad."

My smile faded. "What?"

"Miss Pia and a bad boy biker." Dasia actually giggled under her breath while glancing his way as a bike's engine roared to life. "He's the last guy I could see *you* falling for."

I started toward my car, ignoring the desire to watch him ride off into the night—without me. "And what would be my type of guy?" I couldn't but help ask as his rumbling mufflers faded away.

"A stuffy, dowdy businessman."

"How exciting." Temptation to roll my eyes ended up with sarcasm lacing my voice.

Dasia snorted and tossed her bag onto my back seat. "Exactly."

Rather than focus on her words and what they said about me, I drove us away from the strip joint and did my job of taking her back to the man who, according to her account on the way there, had no right hosting foster kids.

"Give me a few days," I reminded her once more before leaving her with the tearful woman who'd hugged her—and the leering husband beyond with his crossed arms.

I had no choice. And, I hated that truth.

While driving away, my mind returned to Ryker and his bike. His kind offer to help. His checking in with Dasia to make sure she was okay even though I doubted he found my appearance threatening to her in any way. He might appear to be a bad boy biker, but I had a feeling a lot more hid beneath his hardened shell, the exterior of immovability he portrayed. I also wondered what had made him that way, and if there was a way to bring him out of it.

Cursing my nurturing spirit, I returned home to my empty apartment, wishing not for the first time that day I had someone to share it with. Someone with a cold gaze, full beard, and a shaved head I wanted to glide my hands over while wrapping my legs around his waist.

Yes. I had it bad, as Dasia had said.

I also wondered if I'd missed the opportunity of a lifetime to let loose and *breathe* for once.

## 5

## RYKER

It hadn't been the right time or place to ask the pretty little social worker out for a quick fuck to get her out of my system. We hadn't been in the right company—but I sure as fuck had wanted to. A woman like her, though, wouldn't want to just bend over a desk or couch and let me take what I wanted. She'd want the picket fence first. The two-point-five kids and four dogs in exchange. Hugs and cuddles, pillow talk with our bodies all wrapped up. Spooning.

All of which I wasn't capable of offering.

I still found myself in Dunks the next morning, though, hoping she'd show up like she had Friday, even though she hadn't dropped in once prior during the week.

Mom had made it through the night, and I'd promised to bring Jenny a box of Munchkins. Vigil hadn't called, and I could only hope the whole Arturo affair would lay quiet like he did in whatever grave the Vegas Vipers had dug for him.

The beat up Chevy my little social worker had driven off in the night before pulled into the parking lot alongside the window I peered out, and my dick took note quick as fuck, same as it'd done the second I'd caught sight of her in the strip joint.

Tight jeans. Billowy shirt hiding tits my fingers itched to actually touch.

*Goddamnit.*

I shifted to ease the sudden ache in my balls. Jerking off in the shower after getting back to Mom's hadn't eased the load brewing in them one fucking bit.

I needed a warm pussy. Wet mouth. Something other than *me* to get me off.

She walked into Dunks and hesitated right inside the door, scanning the tables to the right where I'd sat on Friday before turning toward the tables on the left.

Our gazes connected, and her lips parted, face flushing. The corner of her lips rose as she offered an unsure wave.

I nodded a greeting of my own even though my lips didn't twitch to reveal the pleasant ... warmth ... radiating through my chest.

She glanced at the counter and back at me as though unsure, another smile lighting her face before she strode toward the young man waiting at the cash register.

My gaze tracked every step, every soft sway of her hips, and the round ass a man could sink his teeth into.

Dick leaking like a salivating mother fucker, I couldn't look away. Didn't fucking want to even though I questioned that tingling in my chest as something so goddamn foreign I couldn't recall feeling it since childhood when my bastard father had actually liked me. Hugged me. Ruffled my hair.

Affection—and my consuming desire for it as a kid.

I cleared my throat, fighting off the need to scowl and flatten the nose I'd done twice before it had doubtless rotted off in a coffin six feet under.

The little lamb got her coffee and turned, attention immediately flitting toward me and the empty chair across the table from where my elbows rested. Her gorgeous tits raised as though she inhaled, pulling in confidence, and strode my way.

"Is this seat taken?"

Goddamn watermelon ... fucking waterworks in my mouth. "Go ahead."

She sat, her hand shaking a bit while setting her purse on the table beside her coffee. "Come here often?" she asked, breathless—and laughed lightly while settling onto the chair. "Sorry. That was really lame."

"Honest question," I told her, taking in the flecks of gold around her slightly dilated pupils. "And to answer it, not really, no. I only stopped by this morning hoping to see you again."

Pink flushed her cheeks. "Oh."

"Ryker McGrath." I held my coffee cup in both hands rather than reach across the table to offer a proper greeting.

"I'm Pia Hill." She smiled wider, her eyes searching my face as though hoping to find some-thing. She didn't offer her hand, either, thank fuck.

"How's your friend?" I lifted my coffee to sip, focus on her expressive eyes.

Pia blinked, her smile faltering. "Dasia. I wish I could say good—but I'm not really sure."

I tucked the young girl's name into my memory. "Tough foster home?"

Her focus slipped to her coffee as she wrapped

her still-trembling hands around it. "You could say that."

"Abuse?"

She lifted her eyes to peer at me, once more seeming to search for something. "That's not exactly something I can talk about, Ryker."

"Who the fuck am I to the situation? What would it hurt? Just making small talk."

She considered for a few seconds and finally nodded. "So she says."

"And you believe her."

"I do, but there's no proof, and he's rich. Her word against his."

I clenched my jaw, glancing around Dunks to try to calm the pissed reaction simmering in my gut. Friends laughing, couples making those goddamn lovey-dovey eyes ... the same damn loud teens from the day before, carefree as fucking birds getting their frou-frou coffees.

"She needs to get out of there," I said, snipping the words out.

"I know." Pia's whisper pulled my focus back to her face. Wetness welled in her eyes. "But it's going to take me a few days to get something else set up for her."

"A few days could be too late."

Pia nodded and swiped at an escaped tear. Not even her own kid, and the woman was all momma-bear toward the girl.

I rubbed at my chest, pushing aside thoughts of my own mom. "What can I do to help?"

She glanced at my leather cut, gaze lingering on the patches on my chest. "While I would love to tell you to go put the fear of God in him—"

"Consider it done." I sat back, hands on my thighs. "Just give me the fucker's name."

Lips pressed together, she tried to suppress a nervous laugh, the wetness in her eyes lessening. "You'll do no such thing. And what happened to just small talk?"

"Who is it, Pia?"

That searching gaze again. She finally shook her head after a few moments of silence while seeming to gather her emotions in check. "I think you want to harm the man."

"Better fucking believe it."

Heavy silence settled between us as she peered at me. "It's a touchy subject for you, isn't it? Something personal."

I stared at her, hating yet appreciating she saw through my hard exterior. Intuitiveness I could admire, even if it earned her my secrets, something only a few of my brothers knew.

Leaning my elbows alongside my coffee, I crowded close as the table allowed. "My sister was raped around the same age as your friend Dasia."

"Did he pay?"

The memory of warm blood coating my hands filled me with sick satisfaction, but I wished I could have done it a dozen times over. "Oh, he paid, alright."

"Good." Pia nodded, not a hint of wariness in her eyes, probably in response to my cold as fuck tone. "I'm glad he's behind bars."

I wasn't about to correct her assumption, but goddamn, what a woman. Sweet, wholesome—with a vindictive side that heated my blood. But he was behind the bars of hell—I nodded anyway.

*Still, not my type,* I reminded myself of the dirty-talking club whores who didn't mind being used without all the promises and gentle caresses a woman like Pia would want.

"I'm sorry for grabbing your arm yesterday morning."

My brow furrowed, but I smoothed it within seconds, still holding her stare. "I don't like to be touched."

"I could tell."

God*damn*, that searching, intuitive gaze...

"Why?"

"Long story," I grumbled, sitting back and grabbing up my coffee again, putting the subject to rest.

She watched me sip, her focus lingering on my lips as I lowered the cup.

Being a little intuitive myself, I knew right where her mind went when I licked the flavor of warm coffee off my lower lip. Her pupils widened slightly, twitching need through my dick again.

"How do you..." Pia tore her focus off my mouth and let out a nervous laugh again, grabbing for her own coffee and hiding behind it while sipping.

"How do I what?" I asked, raising an eyebrow, beyond fucking intrigued by whatever went through her head.

"Sorry. Runaway mouth." Red rushed up from her chest to flush her entire face. "Totally inappropriate," she mumbled, breathless with forced laughter.

I considered for all of two seconds before replying. "Zero intimacy if you're wondering about fucking."

Pia's focus jerked to my face again, blinking as

she digested my blunt words. "You mean you never..."

"I fuck a woman over a piece of furniture when I need to. Otherwise, it's easier just having one of the club whores suck me off without touching me with anything other than her mouth."

Pia stared, lips parted. She hadn't run off—but maybe she should have.

"Sorry." I cleared my throat, realizing how crass I sounded. "I tend to spew shit. There aren't too many sensitive ears around the club."

## 6

## PIA

I should have been offended, not totally turned on, panties soaked and heart beat thumping in my ears. Zero intimacy—zero touching other than fucking a willing, impersonal hole.

*Wow. Just ... wow.*

My mind whirled as fast as the coffee bean grinder in the background. "You could ... um ... always tie a woman up. Keep her from touching you. At least experience the intimacy of doing it face to face. Seeing her eyes when she comes." I snapped my jaw shut, the blood draining from my face as I realized my thoughts spilled out in actual *words*.

*I did not just say that. What the heck is wrong with my filter?*

His cold eyes heated, lighting every inch of my

skin on fire, and I cursed myself for spewing shit like he'd claimed to do seconds earlier. What a mess we were.

"Sorry," I hurried to toss out, same as he'd done. "That was totally inappropriate, too."

"Not a problem. Really." A ghost of a smile twitched his lips, stealing my breath and rushing more wetness to my already soaked panties. "Kinda nice hearing a sweet little girl like you get all nasty and shit."

I let out a shaky laugh instead of the moan wanting to rise from my heaving chest. He'd called me little. And sweet. And, his tone hinted at wanting to corrupt me.

*Just ... wow.*

"So, what are you doing in Southie?" I blurted, my voice tense as hell, needing to calm down already.

"Did your homework since yesterday, I take it?"

"Well." I shrugged, feeling like a sheepish little lamb—the pet name I'd heard him call me at the strip club echoing in my ears all night long while trying to sleep.

"You're a good woman, Pia." The heat in his eyes lowered a few degrees until it blinked out, a wintery gaze taking its place. "You don't want to get involved with a man like me."

Ryker stood and turned as though to walk out without another word, leaving me hanging that quickly. All alone.

"I've always wanted to ride on the back of a Harley," I blurted and snapped my jaw shut again.

He paused and turned, studying me.

"I know you don't like to be touched, but would my holding onto your vest bother you?" I asked, eyeing the leather lying over his chest.

"Cut."

"Huh?"

He grasped the edge of his black leather vest with his free hand, gesturing to the vest with his coffee. "It's called a cut, and to answer your question, I don't know. Never had a woman on the back of my bike before."

His statement echoed in my head, and I waited, breath held as he seemed to consider with his still cool green eyes.

"Got any plans for the day?" he finally asked as though resigned to the fact he wouldn't be rid of me so easily.

I shook my head, trying to find my voice for a change. At least I wasn't spewing shit about wanting to dig into his brain, stir up his pain, and try to heal him of it so he might one day touch me.

"Tell me when and where, and I'll pick you up. Take you for a little ride—see what we both can handle."

I nodded and managed to spit out my apartment address, all-too willing to be aggressive rather than careful like any smart woman. I didn't even know the man.

"Give me your cell." Ryker held out his hand.

I dug it from my purse without thought, handing it to him between two fingers so he wouldn't need to touch me in the exchange.

He took my cell, swiped it on, his fingers flitting over the screen. Seconds later, a muffled ding sounded from somewhere on his person, and he handed my phone back to me.

"I texted my cell," he said. "Let a friend know what you're doing and with who. Give her my number."

I blinked up at him before taking the phone he held out to me, careful to keep our fingers from sliding alongside one another even though I longed for a touch from his calloused hands.

"Okay."

"Two?"

I nodded, having lost my voice again at the thought of tasting freedom in a few hours' time—on a rumbling bike, the bad boy biker looming in front of me close enough I would smell his soap.

His semi-smile reappeared for a flashed second, revamping that fire between my thighs.

"See you soon, little lamb."

Swoon city.

I stared after Ryker as he first grabbed a box of munchkins then strode from Dunks like he owned the building, the damn city, his steps confident and sure.

Determination to heal the sex-on-wheels man flooded through me as quickly as he'd enticed my libido into hyper-drive. He'd been hurt to have such an aversion to touch, and I wanted to heal him.

Crazy, but I didn't just want to—I needed to. Ryker McGrath needed to live again, connect through intimacy he didn't seem to think he missed out on, and I would show him how. Wouldn't hurt to enjoy the hell out of him if given the chance, too.

But until that time, I needed to make some calls and find Dasia a new foster home.

## 7

## RYKER

I lounged on my bed at Mom's, legs stretched out, but booted feet hanging off to the side as requested by my sister. The scent of watermelon lingered in my nose, but I pushed aside thoughts of Pia's glossy lips wrapped around my dick and pulled out my cell.

"Devil," I said the second he answered. "Need you to do something for me."

"Whatcha got, Ryker?"

I gave my tech geek Viper brother all I had— Pia's name and number, the young woman's name she'd saved from the strip joint the night before. Said girl, one Dasia Walker, hadn't been working for Mikey long. He'd been more than willing to cough up her full name for me when I'd stopped by on my way back to Mom's with Jenny's donut holes.

Mikey and I went way back, and he owed me a few favors, anyway. I made sure to assure him he wouldn't catch any shit from anyone for hiring an underage dancer.

"She's a ward of the state," I told Devil. "Need to know who she's staying with."

"Mind my asking why?"

While Devil's fingers clicked on keys in the background, I told him all I knew, all Pia had shared even though it wasn't much. Mikey hadn't known jack shit other than the lies Dasia had put on the application.

Fake ID. Fake address.

"So what's your plan?" Devil asked.

"To kill the fucker."

"Hmm."

I waited, silence on the other end as he worked his magic that couldn't be met by any other acquaintance of mine. Devil should have been head of the fucking CIA. FBI. Had he finished at MIT, he would have been top of his class, no doubt.

"How about we make some money off the fucker instead?" Devil finally said, a hint of smile in his voice.

"Who is it?"

"CEO of Griffey Industries."

"Get the fuck out." I scowled. "Why the fuck is he taking in foster kids?"

"His wife is on a few boards for kid charities." More clicks on the computer. "Shit," Devil huffed. "She's a regular Mother Theresa. You should see all the shit she heads up—fucking donates millions to."

"And her sick fuck of a husband takes advantage —it's why he allows the foster kids in his mansion. Fucking cocksucker."

"No kids of their own... What do you want me to do?" Devil asked while I continued to stew in my disgust and anger.

A soft knock sounded, and Jenny poked her head in the door. "Mind if I run down to the corner store real quick? I'm dying for a box of ice cream."

"Go on. Take a bit of time for yourself. I'll be here until close to two."

"You're a doll," she breathed. The second Jenny shut my door again, my brow furrowed back to its deep groove.

"Tell Vigil everything," I told Devil, my thoughts lingering on my baby sister and the shit she suffered through. "Extort the ever loving fuck out of Griffey, then I'll slit his goddamn throat afterward."

"You got it, brother."

I'd enjoyed the sweet revenge of slicing the throat of the fucker who'd hurt Jenny—and I'd gladly do the same to every pervert who thought to touch too-young, too-innocent girls. Vigilante justice was my fucking reason for living.

Soft-looking blonde hair and searching blue-green eyes with their glints of gold entered my mind.

Having another reason for living would have been nice for a change from the cold hearted callousness ruling my soul. If only I could get over my hatred of touch and every goddamn trigger that set my nerves and stomach on edge when someone touched me without my consent—which I never fucking gave.

## 8

## PIA

My heart pounded in my chest, and I fought off major anxiety as Ryker's bike shot northward on 95, zipping past cars and big trucks alike. I fought the need to squeeze him with my thighs and wrap my arms around him, hanging on for dear life.

What had started with my hands lightly on his sides, our skin separated by his cut and t-shirt, had turned into more a white-knuckled death-grip on that bit of leather, my lifeline to safety. What could be had of it, anyway. At least a helmet protected the top of my head.

I focused on breathing and exhaling to counts of eight, reminding myself of where I sat, how I'd dreamed of doing so, and what my entire body experienced—pure freedom.

The rush of wind, fresh air unhindered by concrete and brick. Eventually, I settled as the miles sped past, releasing tension from one muscle at a time from my head to my toes until I could take stock of my surroundings, enjoy the thunder of the engine. Live the fantasy I'd concocted the morning before.

My smile started out slow, but ended up stretching my face until it hurt, moisture ripping from the corners of my eyes even though I wore sunglasses to protect them from the whipping wind.

I laughed. I couldn't stop the giggles from rising, and I felt an overwhelming urge to lift my hands out to the side, shrieking like a banshee released from the depths of hell.

Euphoria filled me beyond anything I'd felt before, a rush of *life*. Breathing easy. Free. My backside wasn't too happy with the hard leather I sat upon, but in that moment, I didn't care.

The bike slowed as we neared an exit somewhere in New Hampshire, back roads leading us off the highway. Cooler air caressed us easily as we passed through woods, the sun dappled across the black road ahead in bright patches. Kisses of sunlight licked at my face as we meandered through nature, twice the noise of the bike sending squirrels scrambling from the road for safety in the trees.

My hold on Ryker's cut eased a bit, and feeling confident and a bit rebellious, I brushed the inside of my thigh against his outer one as though shifting in my seat.

He didn't react.

A few minutes later, I repeated the action with my left leg as we rounded a bend.

Again, he made no move, not so much as a flinch.

Progress as far as I was concerned. Perhaps touching without skin contact was okay. It would certainly be a better starting point for tearing down his walls.

We'd been on the road for close to three hours, and my ass killed me from sitting on the narrow seat behind Ryker. Numbness crept in until he finally stopped at a small diner in the middle of no-man's land.

Ryker shut the engine off, and the sudden quiet hit me like a full backpack to the side of the head. I slid off the back of his Harley, groaning at the stiffness in my legs and butt.

A smirk lifted his lips as he watched me. "You

alright?"

I grimaced again while flexing my backside in my tight jeans. "I think so." I grabbed a handful of my flesh and kneaded, lifting first one knee than the other, trying to stretch out a bit.

Ryker actually chuckled, the sound lighting me up inside and warming me through. "Hungry?" he asked.

I bit my tongue before spewing the sudden thought about wanting a taste of *him*.

His gaze darkened with lust as he stood, though, his focus on my face and probably catching my thought. "A look like that will get you in a whole lotta trouble, little lamb."

I gulped, imagining myself tied up and at his mercy, an impersonal hole for him to take however he wished.

*Wow. I should not be turned on by that...*

"After you, little lamb," he said with another chuckle, motioning toward the diner.

Trying to grasp hold of my raging hormones and cursing my soaked panties, I strode toward the restaurant, clueless how the evening would play out.

I'd been unable to do a damn thing for Dasia, and had decided I needed to enjoy my time away without worrying my poor fingernails to death like

I'd have done otherwise if I'd sat at home all night long. Alone.

Ryker had offered escape in more ways than one, and the desire to take advantage of every second, every experience offered, pushed me forward.

The only waitress in the place took our order for burgers and fries, and Ryker turned his full focus on me, leaning onto the table with his elbows, his eyes more green than hazel in the sunlight shining through the window beside us.

"What are you doing here, Pia?"

"Enjoying the hell out of my life for a change," I replied with a full-on grin, fingering the flatware on their cheap paper napkin. "Even with a sore as hell backside, I've never felt so liberated. All that fresh air." I outright laughed and glanced around the fifties-themed diner with its old vinyl records and pin-up girls plastered to the walls. "I wanted to throw my hands out to the sides and laugh my ass off."

Ryker still watched my mouth when I turned back toward him, the left side of his curling a bit in a half-smirk.

The tingles between my thighs intensified, and I squeezed them together, needing to ease the ache. "I love your smile," I blurted, my face heating as I jerked my focus back up to his eyes.

"I don't do it much, but there's something about you..."

I raised an eyebrow, butterflies having the time of their life inside my stomach. "What?" I couldn't help but ask, sounding all breathless and needy.

He took his time studying my face as though memorizing every line, every angle. Did he think about caressing my cheek? Kissing my lips?

"You're a beautiful woman, Pia," he finally said. "Wholesome with a side of naughty I'm not even sure you're aware of."

"My inappropriate word spewage, you mean," I said with an embarrassed laugh.

"Yeah. I like that shit."

My smile widened, my face and body warmer than a microwaved diet meal for one.

"It's one thing hearing a club whore talk like that, but a woman like you?" Ryker tipped his head to the side, his smirk returning. "Hot as fuck."

My breath left in a rush as sexual energy rippled between us. I wanted to climb over the table into his lap, rip at his beard and eat at his mouth, drinking in his breath, his taste. *Him.*

"Goodness." I fanned my face, forcing my attention off his intense stare to the silent juke box in the corner and the only other couple in the restaurant sitting beside it.

"While I want you to feed more of my fantasies with your word spewage," he said, "I find myself wanting to know you—what other secret parts you hide beneath that motherly nature and conservative clothes."

I hesitated, completely thrown off my guard. The few men I'd dated over the years hadn't been interested in me beyond seeing and feeling up what I hid by my clothes. No one had ever mentioned my protective drive to care for innocents—but Ryker had picked up on that part of my personality. Honed in on it, even, wanting to know more about it rather than my thoughts on being tied up and used.

"Wow. Um ... okay. What do you want to know?"

"Anything." His gaze lightened as he sat back to allow our waiter to set our drinks in front of us. "Everything," he said as she walked off once more.

I held my straw and took a sip of tonic, the bubbles burning down my suddenly dry esophagus as I considered where to start—and what all to share without revealing personal information no one else needed to know.

"I grew up in foster care, too."

Ryker nodded as though unsurprised by my confession.

"And after having experienced that life, I knew I wanted to make childhood a better experience for all the other young, lonely souls feeling they don't have a place in this world."

"So, you've always been good-hearted."

I shrugged. "Pretty much. I never rebelled, and I studied hard in school since I wanted more for my life than I'd been dealt."

"Tell me more."

I did, keeping from the unsavory bits of being a foster kid, turning the focus on him and his background as often as possible. An hour flew by as we spoke, sharing our thoughts on politics, philosophy, and life.

The usual get to know you stuff people enjoy while out on a first date. We saw eye to eye in all things that mattered, right down to climate change and the fact most politicians didn't give two shits—his words, not mine—even though I agreed wholeheartedly.

We'd finished up slices of homemade apple pie and coffee when my cell rang. I didn't recognize the number, but I rarely did when so many clients and foster families had my number.

"Miss Pia, it's Dasia."

My heart stalled out even though her voice sounded fine. "Are you okay?" I blurted, straightening in my chair as Ryker's brow furrowed.

"Yes. I'm at my friend's house—this is her cell number."

"Did you run away again? Did anything happen?"

"No and kinda."

My breath caught at the hesitation in Dasia's voice. Ryker's scowl deepened. "What happened?" I asked, my motherly tone firm.

"I've been putting my desk chair under my doorknob at night, and he tried to get in an hour after we all went to bed."

"Nothing happened, though?" I asked.

"No," Dasia said with a heavy exhale. "If he'd have forced his way in, he would have made enough noise to wake his Stepford wife."

My mind scrambled for a way to keep her safe, but she went on before a lightbulb went off above my head.

"I'm staying here at Stacey's tonight."

"Do your foster parents know where you are?"

"Mrs. Griffey knows," Dasia said. "Told me it was

fine since she knows Stacey's parents and confirmed where I was with her mom."

I let out a heavy breath, sinking back into my chair, and attempted a smile at Ryker to ease the tension seeming to ride his shoulders and the poor skin between his eyebrows. My thumb tingled to reach out and smooth the skin.

"I appreciate your calling me, Dasia."

"Yeah—I just wanted you to know so you wouldn't have to worry about me tonight. I know how you get."

My smile came easy. "I would love you like my own if I could."

"I know, Miss Pia." Music suddenly blared in the background. "Stacey started the movie," Dasia said, "so I gotta go."

"Enjoy yourself," I blurted, excited she would be able to rest easy for one night at least.

"Why don't you look up that badass biker and take a night off from worry yourself?" she said with a laugh.

I smiled, butterflies returning to dance in my stomach as my gaze returned to Ryker's face—his intense stare. "Maybe I will."

"Good. You need to get laid."

"Dasia Walker!" Heat shot up and over my chest.

She giggled—and hung up.

"She alright?" Ryker asked as I set my cell on the table, my hand a bit shaky.

"She's staying with a friend, but he tried to break into her room last night and failed."

His lips flatlined, and he pulled a couple of twenties from his pocket, tossing them onto the table. "Ready to roll?"

My backside wasn't so sure, but the sudden freedom of nagging worry in the back of my head had me wanting to toss my arms out wide again— and maybe tighten my thighs a bit around his while jetting down the road.

"Let's ride," I told him with a grin.

9

———

**RYKER**

We made the three hour trip southward as the sun set to our right sending streaks of red across the sky. Until we arrived back at Pia's apartment, darkness hovered above, any pinpricks of starlight hidden by the city's lights.

Pia had pushed a bit on the ride back, her thighs brushing against my outer ones when unnecessary. Hardly by chance, too. While I'd fought off the need to flinch since we flew down a highway, the touch through clothing didn't clench my stomach into knots like skin contact did.

My dick fucking loved it, that was for damn sure. Fucking thing strained for release, smearing pre-cum inside my leathers like I hadn't experienced since being a young punk checking out Mrs.

Flaherty, our neighbor who'd loved to garden in crop tops and Daisy Duke's.

I parked and cut the engine even though Pia hadn't invited me in—but I had high fucking hopes and blue balls for fucking days.

"Coming in?" she asked, her face flushed in her apartment building's flood lights as she climbed off the back of my bike. She grimaced and rubbed her ass.

"I don't have good intentions," I told her the truth.

Her lips parted on an intake of air. "Meaning you want me tied up, bent over my couch, or on my knees, hands behind my back?" She slapped a hand over her mouth, that sexy as hell flush taking over her cheeks.

"Goddamnit, woman," I growled, my dick jerking.

She shoved her hands in her back pockets, her flirty smile showing off her dimple and sending that new rush of warmth through my chest again.

She popped out one lush hip, propping her hand on it with unpracticed fumbling. Fucking adorable. "Do I need to ask twice?"

I climbed off my bike without taking my eyes off her face. Her smile faded as I loomed, need to order her to her knees barely suppressed. As much as I wanted to bury my dick balls deep inside her sweet pussy to get my rocks off, I found I didn't want to be an asshole with her. "I can take what I want, what you think *you* want, Pia, but I can't give you what you need."

"What I need," she said, her voice breathless and rushed, "is for you to take what you want, Ryker. Use me for your pleasure. Show me that darkness inside your soul."

*Fuck. Me.*

Pia didn't know what she asked for, but I wasn't about to deny her. Given the green fucking light, I nodded toward the apartment building, and she turned, hurrying forward and digging a key out of her pocket.

Every sway of her hips led me on like a fucking dog on a leash, desperate to shove my face in her ass and sniff.

It'd been a long fucking time since I'd attempted to taste a woman in that way—hadn't ended well for either of us when she'd reached back to grasp my hair.

Teeth clenched, I forced the memory back in the black dungeon inside my head, slamming the door shut with finality. Along with it, I made sure to lock up my heart, my emotions. Pia tempted my vulnerability to within a goddamn inch of my life.

First floor apartment—small from a quick glance at the living area and kitchen to the right.

The couch lay straight ahead, the back a perfect height.

*Did she expect a bit of foreplay—*

The thought cut off from my mind as she bent to unlace her boots, ass in the air, wide and juicy, her jeans tight against flesh I actually *wanted* to pound against rather than fight to ignore while fucking into a wet hole.

*Goddamn.* I grasped my dick through my leathers, trying to calm the fuck down.

Pia straightened and tossed a glance over her shoulder, catching me with my hand on my dick.

"See something you want?" she asked, once more breathless and shaky.

"Fuck, yes," I growled. "Take off your jeans."

She kept her back to me, her focus over her shoulder on my face while doing as told, shimmying them down her legs.

The sight of pale pink panties—not quite virginal but far from sexy—brought a deep groan up from my chest. "Slide those off, too," I said, my voice rasped to fucking hell from lust to bust a nut.

Again, she did as I said, shimmying the scrap of cotton down over her smooth-looking, pale legs. Wetness darkened the lining. Hadn't once buried my face in a woman's pussy, but I sure as hell enjoyed the scent of one. I breathed in deep, hoping to catch a whiff of her musk.

No such fucking luck.

"Toss them to me," I told her, letting go of my dick to hold out my hand.

Pink fused across her face as she turned a bit to flip her panties toward me.

Gaze glued to the patch of blonde curls between her thighs, I buried my nose in her warm panties and breathed deep, sucking her into my lungs. Watermelon and musk. *Holy fucking mother of God—* saliva burst from every goddamn gland in my mouth, and I swallowed back another groan.

"Tell me you're ready for me, Pia," I muttered into the cotton before sniffing again.

Her head jerked up and down.

"Touch yourself. Show me."

She audibly gulped, and I stared as she slid her fingers down over her pubic bone, into the hidden heaven below. A whimper, and she pulled her fingers back upward, wetness glistening on one digit up to the second knuckle.

"Suck it clean," I ordered, my voice uneven. Harsh with anger over the fact I couldn't do it my goddamn self.

I watched the finger disappear between her plump lips and her cheeks hollow out while sucking it clean.

"Tell me what you taste like, little lamb."

Pia licked her lower lip after removing her finger from her mouth as though hoping to catch the last bit of lingering flavor. "Tangy."

"Sweet?"

She shrugged, red across her heaving chest and up her neck.

"You've never tasted yourself before."

"No."

I reached down and unbuttoned my leathers, shoving them down far enough to spring my leaking dick free.

Pia licked her lower lip again, and I grasped my base, squeezing to keep from blowing like a goddamn wet-behind-the-ears teen from her stare alone.

"Have you tasted *your*self?" she whispered.

I considered lying, but found I didn't want to. "Yeah. Salty as shit—I don't know why women like it."

She lifted her focus off my dick to my face, her hands clenching and unclenching at her sides. "Can I taste you?" she whispered, sending another welling of pre-cum to dribble down toward my hand.

Her mouth would feel like fucking heaven—but I didn't trust the shaking hands at her sides. She seemed the touchy-feely type.

"Bend over the couch, Pia," I told her, fishing a condom from my back pocket. I didn't carry the fucking things too often, but I'd come prepared—just in case she wasn't turned off by what I wanted.

She stared, lips slightly parted as I sheathed my dick.

"Over the couch," I repeated, "legs spread."

A shiver rippled down over her body, raising goose bumps along her legs, and she turned away, draping her body over the couch's back.

"Hands behind your head," I said, stepping closer, my focus snagged by the pink folds and wetness smeared along the insides of her thighs. Fucking soaked, and I hadn't even touched her.

*Goddamn, what a sweet little lamb.*

Her clasped fingers turned white knuckled behind her head before I stepped in close enough to rub the tip of my dick up through her slick wetness.

"Oh..." She shuddered but kept her hands in place.

I notched and released my hold on my dick to grasp the back of the couch beside her hips. While I wouldn't be able to help my pelvis and the tops of my thighs from slamming against her soft skin, I knew the clasp of her pussy sucking me in would be enough to keep my stomach from turning.

She moaned as I pressed forward, and I fought the need to blow early while watching my dick disappear inside her tight heat.

"Holy fuck." I clenched my teeth, head tipped back as I bottomed out, the feel of her warm ass cheeks against my pelvis almost as much a fucking turn on as her pussy squeezing my dick. I'd never in my life felt that. Ever.

My neck strained, and I dug my fingers into the couch while fighting for calm and gliding back out, dragging my dick along her slick walls.

Pia whimpered and shifted beneath me as I slowly pressed back in. "Ryker..."

She whispered my name on a choked sob, and I jerked my eyelids open to make sure her hands remained clasped.

"Too much?" I asked through clenched teeth as my dick pressed against her cervix.

"More."

"Fuck." I pulled out and shoved back in with enough force Pia squeaked—and moaned again. Most women couldn't get off with a little clit play, and most of the club whores didn't even try when letting me take what I needed.

But Pia...

She whimpered and moaned, every noise escaping her like a double shot of espresso to my drawn up balls.

I wasn't going to last—and I wanted to feel her come around me. I wanted her cum dripping off my balls, creaming up the hell out of my cock.

"Touch your clit." I slid out fully, my dick aching —jerking to sink back into the swollen pinkness holding my attention. "I want to feel you come around me, little lamb."

She kept one hand behind her head and sneaked the other between her thighs and the couch, her legs trembling. "Put it back in, Ryker," she pleaded, sounding near tears while working her clit, her hips gyrating, seeking release. "Please."

I speared in without notching first, and she convulsed. "Ryker!" Her breath caught, and her pussy squeezed the living fuck out of my thrusting dick. Our skin slapped together as I plowed into her pulsing channel over and over, tingles rising up from my toes as wetness smeared between us, dripping off my balls to the floor.

"Fuck, little lamb." I groaned as the first spurt of cum shot from my dick into its rubber prison, my fingers in a vise on the couch as my ass flexed without rhythm, desperate to empty my balls. One last dribble of cum, and I stilled, buried deep, heaving for breath, the scent of sweat, sex, and watermelon overwhelming my goddamn brain.

I cursed a few more times while catching my breath, finally taking note of her softness still holding my semi, the wetness of her cum, the warmth of her ass still pressed against my groin.

For the first time in my life, I didn't back out quick as fuck after finishing.

Groaning, I slid out, grasping the base of the condom to keep it in place, actually missing the feel of her warm skin against mine. "Bathroom?" I asked, wondering over the sudden weakness in my legs as she sighed, her hand hanging lax between her spread legs.

"Back of the hall on the left," she whispered, her tone hinting at a smile.

"You alright?" I asked before moving away.

"Never been better," she replied on a sigh, lifting

her head to peer over her shoulder at me. "That was fucking hot."

My lips twitched at the curse word on hers, and my dick attempted to swell again at the flush on her face, the sated sleepiness in her eyes.

"Be right back," I said rather than reach out to caress the gorgeous globes of her ass like my fingers itched to do.

A few minutes later, I exited the bathroom to find Pia unmoved. I pressed the warm, wet towel I'd brought along for her against her inner thigh, and she sighed, thankfully lifting her still dangling hand to care for what I couldn't.

"Don't leave yet," she said, vulnerability in her eyes when she finally stood and looked my way.

"I won't." I'd tucked my dick away, telling myself we were done for the night. A woman's ass hadn't ever felt so goddamn good—hadn't *ever* felt good to the point I wanted more than the wet hole between.

A muscle in my jaw ticked as my gaze lingered on Pia's backside while she walked a bit shakily to the bathroom. At the click of the door, I slumped on the couch and closed my eyes, tipping my head back where I'd gripped minutes earlier, lost in lust, lost in need.

Fucking lost in Pia.

Best feeling ever. Also, scariest fucking thing I'd ever experienced. I couldn't deny wanting more, but not just getting off. I wanted more of her, her thoughts, her laughter, her dimple.

Wanting led to heartache, though. The need for physical affirmation would leave me grasping, hopeless, and hurting.

"Fuck." I scrubbed a hand down over my face, pulling on the end of my beard as the whiskers slid against my palm.

Pia joined me a few minutes later—I couldn't bear the thought of leaving out of fear, hurting her when she'd asked me to stay.

Sleep shorts and a thin tank top covered her curves from my roaming gaze, and barely at that.

My dick took note of the hardened nipples of her large breasts, and for the first time in my life, I wondered what it felt like to fuck a pair of tits like hers rather than just get myself off to watching another guy do it on some porn site.

I cleared my throat and forced my attention on her face as she settled on the couch, sideways, her knee mere inches from my thigh. Rigidity kept me in place, my stomach knotted and palms sweating even though I'd been balls deep inside her body minutes earlier.

"Are you okay?" she whispered, and I shied away from the hand she reached toward mine atop my thigh. "Sorry."

I nodded as she pulled her hand back.

"My father was my hero when I was young," I heard myself toss out what few of my Viper brothers knew. I wanted her to know the truth. Every goddamn bit of it. "Used to carry me everywhere, hug and kiss me. Ruffle my hair." I swallowed against the tightness in my throat I hadn't experienced for years when remembering the better days of my childhood.

"I fucking thrived on his affection—more so than my mom's. I lived for his words of edification, his touch that assured me of his love. Drank it down like a parched little bastard."

"When did he stop?" Pia asked when I paused.

I lifted my focus off my lap I hadn't realized I'd moved off her in the replays from my mind.

Her intuitive stare held me transfixed.

"When Mom came home from the hospital with Jenny."

Pia waited while my stomach twisted over revealing that truth I hadn't told anyone.

I fucking spilled, spewed out the shit of my childhood—the heartache of losing my father's love and attention, gaining the drunken wrath from hands that had once gently consoled and showed love.

"I'm a fucked up, callous bastard, Pia," I said, still unmoving on her couch, my focus once more on my hands.

"I wondered over your childhood," she finally said. "I've seen a lot of kids experience similar things you did. Makes it easier for me to spot."

A dry huff of laughter moved my lips as she shifted, her knee close as fuck to my leg. "Even in an old fuck like me?"

"You're not old."

"I'm forty-three," I said, finally meeting her gaze again after spilling my baggage in a vomit of bad memories.

"Oh." She smirked, her gaze caressing my face and settling on my lips.

"What?"

"I'm thirty-three."

A once pure, wholesome woman of thirty-three who'd allowed a criminal, a murderer, between her thighs without a single touch of foreplay.

"How'd I entice a good woman like you to bend over a goddamn couch?" I grumbled, although thankful as fuck.

She lifted her hand and feathered a fingertip over my lower lip before I could react.

My breath caught, and I jerked backward from the sear of energy racing over my entire face.

"Sorry!" She clasped her hands on her lap and swallowed, her eyes wide. "I'm so sorry," she repeated, "I didn't mean to, but I really like you ... you make me feel ... alive."

"That was the bike ride." I tossed the words out, hoping to ease the tension crushing my chest.

Pia laughed, the sound doing more to soothe the anxiety that had rushed over me at her touch than my flippant remark had done.

"I'll take you for a ride whenever the fuck you want, little lamb," I heard myself say—and I meant every fucking word, fragile heart in my chest I didn't know I still owned be damned.

## 10

## PIA

**H**oly wow.

Ryker hadn't touched me with more than his cock and groin area—and I'd never had better. I yearned for more with a deep ache beyond lust. That moth to flame crap hadn't ever been truer in my mind.

I wanted to curl in his lap and listen to his heartbeat. I wanted to cuddle in bed, our limbs entwined, lips touching and tasting. Needed both like my hands and heart needed to offer the affection he obviously still craved but shielded himself from.

He claimed he couldn't give me what I needed, but we'd made progress, though, and I wasn't one to give up easily.

For two hours, we talked, late into the night.

Knowing Dasia lay safe in a bed far away from her foster father eased my mind and allowed me freedom I hadn't realized I'd been missing out on.

For years.

I managed to brush against a clothed part of Ryker a few times in those hours, and he didn't shy away like he had when I'd instinctively touched his soft lips.

"Is it just skin on skin?" I finally asked after about the third time I bumped his leg with my knee while rearranging myself on the couch.

"It's easier to ignore the PTSD when there's something between my skin and another person, yeah," he said with a shrug.

He pretended nonchalance about quite a bit, but I wasn't fooled by his feigned bravery or hardened heart.

I wondered over the sleeping teddy bear inside him, the one his father had smothered and laid to rest thirty-some years earlier. With the way his gaze lingered on my lips and my chest, I expected he longed to touch—just couldn't get over his fear of rejection.

"Can we try?" I asked, the side of my head rested against the back of the couch as I faced him.

He gave me a side eye but without a trace of annoyance. "Try what?"

"Me touching you—through your clothes."

The tension rolled off him like fog off a can of dry ice, shivering over my skin.

"It's okay," I whispered, hating the disappointment stinging my heart. "I can do without."

*For now.*

A yawn cracked my jaw, tearing up my eyes, and I glanced at the clock on the wall. Two in the morning. I giggled. "I haven't been up this late since college. You're a bad influence on me, Ryker McGrath."

"Don't I know it." Ryker exhaled and stretched his neck side to side. "I ought to get going."

"Stay." The offer flew from my lips without thought, but I knew as I said the single word, I didn't want anything more. The thought of being alone in the apartment I'd spent over two years in nearly choked off my air.

He hesitated, giving me hope. "I've never slept in bed with a woman."

"My bed is plenty big for both of us," I rushed to spew, grasping at straws. "One side for you, one side for me. The pillow on the opposite side of mine is always unruffled when I wake every morning. Promise."

We studied one another in the soft lamplight I'd turned on in place of the overhead lights.

"I've always wondered—" Ryker snapped his jaw shut, his eyes taking on that shut-off glaze I didn't like.

"So, let's go find out." I hopped up and strode back down the hallway before he could argue or make excuses, hoping he'd follow me like he'd done when I'd invited him into my apartment.

I plumped the unused pillows and pulled back the blankets on the left side of my bed, keeping focus on the bedroom doorway in my periphery.

Ryker filled it as I moved around the foot of my king sized bed to ready my own side.

"That's a big fucking bed."

"I like my space," I stated, pulling back my covers, not about to tell him I moved around a lot in my sleep even if I didn't touch the extra pillow. That would definitely send him out the door.

I slid off my shorts, and bit back a smirk as he groaned when I lifted my tank off overhead. My breasts swayed as I leaned down to crawl into bed, and he cursed under his breath.

"Hit the lights before you crawl in here," I told

him, closing my eyes and scooting down a bit into the soft mattress cradling my body.

Silence.

Another curse.

The light switch flicked off.

A minute later, my ears strained in the darkness as clothing rustled. My bed dipped, the tension in the body on the far side radiating over toward me.

"Ryker."

"Hmm?" he grunted.

"Are you naked?"

"Yeah."

Warmth grew between my thighs, and I breathed in the clean scent of his soap wafting off his body a mere two feet or so away. "Too hot?" I asked.

"I'm good."

I sighed, telling myself to sleep, but I couldn't think about anything but his naked body, and how good he'd felt thrusting deep inside mine. My nipples ached as the warmth turned to wetness, coating my panties.

"Ryker?"

"Hmm?" he grunted again.

I sighed again, knowing that pushing could very well mess up the progress we'd made. "Thank you for today."

"My pleasure, little lamb."

Hoping we could pick up where we'd left off in the morning, I rolled to face the wall, giving him the space he needed. After maybe ten minutes of tense silence while I replayed his bending over my couch, I still couldn't sleep.

"Ryker?" I said, rolling onto my back again.

"Hmm?" he questioned, not sounding tired in the least or annoyed I bugged him.

"Turn on the light."

The bed shifted as he rolled toward the bed stand and my lone lamp. A click brightened the room, and I blinked my eyes to adjust.

He rolled back toward me, and we studied one another from the short distance separating us.

I wanted to spew out the words about being horny, wanting his cock, the wetness between my thighs, but bit my tongue. Never in my life had I been such a forward, randy woman, desperate for a man's touch.

"What's on your mind, little lamb?"

"You."

"And?"

"Me."

A smirk lifted the corner of his lips, and I nearly swooned at the rush of arousal swelling through me.

"Use your words like a big girl," Ryker said, heat growing in his steady gaze.

"I want you to fuck me again."

"Goddamn." He groaned and eyed my headboard. "Think you can grab hold and not let go?"

I shimmied off my panties fast as a cop chasing down a criminal and shoved down the blankets to bare myself, fully intending to roll onto my knees and stick my ass into the air for his taking.

"No."

I paused on one knee, my brow furrowing as he rolled on a condom he'd fished from his pants on the floor.

Ryker swallowed, his focus unwavering from my face. "I want to watch you when you come around my dick, Pia."

A rush of tenderness and absolute delicious need rolled over me and stole my breath.

I laid back and grasped the headboard's bars, hoping like hell—praying even—I could keep my hands firmly locked in place. Not seeing his face while bent over the couch had made it easier to keep from reaching out. Touching. Feeling warmth and familiarizing my hands with every dip and ridge of his body.

He rose to his knees, focus slipping down over

my prone, shivering form, and I drank in my fill of hard muscle, pecs, and abs I hadn't expected for his age, silly me and my lack of knowledge concerning the male body. Tattoos scattered across his torso. The shaft already swollen between his powerful looking thighs.

He moved in close, and I didn't dare twitch a muscle, didn't even arch as he pressed into my more than ready body. My arms shook, breath stuttered, heart thundered, but I kept my shaking thighs wide to keep from touching him too much.

His eyes shown greener than I'd noted before, with an intensity that rushed adrenaline through me and arousal to seep around his buried cock. He set his hands on the mattress by my shoulders, dragged out, pulling a whimper from me, and thrusting back in to catch my breath again.

I set my feet on the mattress—couldn't help myself—and lifted to meet him on the next thrust.

"Goddamn," he said through clenched teeth, his gaze dipping down between us where our bodies joined.

The scent of sex, the sounds of very *wet* sex, enveloped me in heat that rushed through me from head to toes. I lost myself in his eyes, and when he buried deep and ground his pelvis against me, my climax arched my back, brushing my chest against him—and he grunted, filling the condom rather than me like I suddenly wished he'd done.

———

A vibrating buzz woke me, and I blinked open one eye to find a hint of light around my shades—and a heavy limb over one of my spread legs.

Hot breath fanned the side of my face, and I held still while fully waking with realization we'd cuddled a bit while sleeping.

The buzz came again, and Ryker shifted, his semi-hard ridge brushing against my thigh.

*Oh...*

I wanted to press into him, wrap my hand around his length, feel the satiny skin, swipe at a bead of pre-cum—

Ryker tensed at the third buzz. "Fuck." He ripped his leg away from mine and rolled to the edge of the bed, leaning over to fish in what I assumed to be his clothes.

Cell in hand, he sat up once more. "Jenny?"

I shifted onto my side, hands beneath my pillow to keep from soothing the ridged set of his shoulders as he listened to his sister. He ran a hand over his scalp, his calloused palm scratching at the hint of stubble he must shave off every morning.

"Fuck," he said again, grabbing up his pants. "I'll be there in twenty."

I scrambled to sit as he yanked on his leathers, his back still toward me. Lifting the sheet over my bare chest kept my hands from reaching for him to soothe whatever hurt I could feel rolling off him in waves.

"Ryker?"

"Mom died in her sleep."

Nonchalant, but hardly flippant—but he didn't fool me. He'd told me she lived on borrowed time, that the hospice nurses didn't expect her to make it much past the weekend.

Sunday, a day of rest, and I knew he would do no such thing.

"I'm sorry," I whispered as he pulled his t-shirt down over his head. "Can I do anything to help?"

He shook his head and sat once more to pull on his sock and boots. "I appreciate the offer, but no."

Worrying the inside of my lip, I watched him finish dressing and grab up his cut off the foot of the bed. He finally paused and faced me.

He'd hardened his eyes, shutting me out from whatever emotions he experienced. "Thank you for that," he said, motioning toward my bed with his chin. "I'm glad I got to experience that first with you."

"Did it upset you?" I asked, keeping a close watch on his face. "Waking up with our legs touching?"

A muscle in his jaw twitched his beard. "A little."

"Maybe we can try again sometime." My suggestion came out needier sounding that I'd wanted, but he nodded, keeping me from crushing disappointment.

"I'll give you a call."

*Said every man to their one night stands*, I heard in my head as he strode out the door of my bedroom, disappearing into the hallway. My ears strained for his boots on tile as he passed through the kitchen and into the tiny foyer. The front door clicked shut quietly behind him, and I sank back into bed, my eyes closing, my heart aching.

Not being able to offer comfort when a person needed it really sucked. Not knowing how he felt about me sucked even harder.

11
———

## RYKER

I hadn't expected one goddamn ounce of grief over Mom's passing, but I'd be lying if I said it didn't hurt at all. The fact I couldn't even fucking hug my sister—she wrapped her arms around herself while the coroner rolled Mom's body out the condo's door—pissed me the hell off.

The need to punch the shit out of something, demolish a face, shed some blood, rode my shoulders tense to the point I caved and poured myself three shots of whiskey before focusing on the shit I needed to take care of.

A call to my lawyer later that morning set paperwork in motion. A call to Vigil let him know I'd be staying in Southie for at least another two days.

We didn't plan a wake or funeral, just a simple

incineration of Mom's body and a vat of ashes I had no wish to see or touch. Jenny would keep the memento or whatever the shit one called a jar of burned human flesh and bone—I didn't give a fuck what she did with them.

Tuesday afternoon, I took to the open road, high-tailing it up North 95 toward home. I'd wanted to call Pia to let her know I was leaving Southie, but couldn't bring myself to do it.

Waking to find my leg over hers, my bare dick against her soft thigh had fucked with my head. I'd wanted more. Wanted to roll her beneath me, demand she wrap her legs around me, dig her fingernails into me, rip at my hair and my beard while I fucked us both raw.

*Goddamnit.*

My dick swelled in my leathers, the rumbling vibrations of my bike beneath me making me harder than hell.

I wanted more. Wanted *her*.

Fear clawed at the back of my mind, even as lust to sink balls deep into her sweet pussy while she wrapped herself around me, filled my head. Fucking war—and I needed another drink.

I drove straight to the club, parked, and stalked

inside, nearly slamming the door against the wall as I strode through the entryway.

"Ryker!" Vigil called from the end of the bar, and I shot him a scowl. "Pour the man a shot," he told the prospect manning the bar after a glance at my face. "Leave the bottle."

I sat on the stool beside Vigil and nodded at the prospect who hooked me up. Two shots burned their way to my guts before I felt I could breathe again.

"How are you doing, brother?"

"Fucking fine as fuck," I muttered, pouring myself a third, my dick at least a half-mast rather than raging and leaking.

"Got shit taken care of?"

"Yep." I slammed back my third, ready for oblivion to take away the goddamn emotions hurdling over me like a bunch of fucking gazelles intent on escaping a lion.

We sat in silence as I sucked down whiskey, one shot after another.

Devil joined us for a time, offering condolences —but Stone and Warden along with their old ladies didn't show, thank fuck. Couldn't handle seeing that shit when I couldn't get Pia out of my head.

I crashed on Vigil's couch in his office rather than

attempt to drive home, too damn drunk to care about the stench of the old piece of shit and the dozens of old cum stains from past fucks on its cushions.

Darkness finally took over my mind, my emotions, and I rested for the first time in forty-eight hours.

The next morning, a few brothers and prospects were in the club when I stumbled out into the land of the living. No one bothered checking in with me or even greeting me for that matter as I stalked through the club intent on the door. I expect my scowl kept them away.

Once home, I showered and relieved the ache in my balls, but once finished and dressed again, I took note of the heavy silence inside my house. Three bedrooms, two of which sat empty of anything. A large eat-in kitchen and nice den I'd spent some cash to outfit with leather sofas, a big fucking TV for football season right around the corner, and a loaded liquor cabinet in the corner.

I eyed the bottle of whiskey, but my stomach churned. The amber liquid disappeared down the goddamn drain while I swore to never drink the shit again.

Slapping a steak on the grill appealed more, so I did just that—and sat alone at my table, wondering why I suddenly couldn't stand the quiet. The peace of being alone.

I called Klingon an hour later, expecting he'd finally be up and around out in Vegas.

"Fuck, man, sorry to hear that, brother," he said when I told him about Mom. While he'd had a better childhood than I did, he'd always had a soft spot for my mom even when I didn't.

"Met a woman," I blurted out the next bit of news and clenched my eyes shut tight at my stupidity.

"The fuck?"

I snorted. "Not gonna ask me how that's working out?" He knew exactly what I'd meant—and fucking laughed.

"She must not be the clingy type."

"Fuck off," I clipped my words, the sudden need to defend Pia catching me off guard. "She's a good woman. Social worker with a heart of fucking gold."

"She'll need one to put up with your ass."

"Fuck off," I repeated.

He laughed louder, his voice booming through my cell phone. "You gonna use more than your dick to touch the poor woman?"

"I want to."

Klingon sobered quick as fuck, silence settling. "Yeah?" he finally asked.

"Fucking crave it." Tremors began in my legs, creeping up my body, settling in my chest as I considered my statement. "I want her hands on me," I admitted, feeling a little better over letting that truth out.

"You should go see a shrink, Ryk," Klingon said, and my brow went back to its deep furrowed state.

The last thing I needed to do was sit down and spill the shit of my life—and end up rotting my ass off in prison. No fucking way would a moral man keep his mouth shut after learning all I'd done since learning the difference between right and wrong.

"Baby steps."

"What?" I asked, confused as fuck and staring at my black TV screen.

"Take baby steps," Klingon said. "A little touch at a time. Through clothes until you can handle it, then move on to more when you're comfortable."

"You going all psychologist on my ass?"

"Nah. Just seemed like a good idea."

"And if it doesn't work?"

"Won't know if you don't fucking try."

I changed the topic to assholes sniffing around

about the shit show we'd created, but he assured me no one had.

I considered Klingon's words about baby steps long after we hung up, but I was still too chicken shit to call Pia.

## 12

## PIA

Ryker hadn't called since his mom had passed, and I fought off the desire to wallow in self-pity, thinking I'd been nothing but a bitch to get his rocks off with. Replaying the conversations we'd had through my head kept me in the game, though. We'd connected on a few levels from coffee to lasagna, from pot roast to the Patriots.

But I liked cats—he liked dogs.

I enjoyed frou-frou drinks. He preferred beer and shots of whiskey even though he claimed he wanted to quit both—I expected his father influenced those wishes, too.

I liked to dive deep into emotions and what triggers them. He avoided admitting to what he felt beyond lust and anger.

I wondered over his emotional state and the lack of grief I'd noted on his face when he'd gotten off the phone with his sister Jenny. While I knew he didn't have a good relationship with his mom from the bits of his childhood he'd shared with me, I didn't understand the cold heartedness that had frozen his face over learning of her death.

Had he mourned at all? Did he still?

My heart ached to hold him, tell him it was okay for a badass biker man to show feelings. Keeping them all bottled up inside wasn't good for anyone—especially a person who might piss him off by accident and reap the consequences.

I also wondered about Dasia and how she fared at the Griffey's. I hadn't heard from her, and worry nagged my insides Tuesday night. Deciding I needed to focus on what I *could* influence, I called the Griffey's landline. Dasia's foster mother answered and told me she would let Dasia know I wished to speak with her.

Warm voice, sweet as southern peach pie—Mrs. Griffey truly was a loving woman. If only she knew about her husband's liking for girls he had no business—or right—touching.

"Hey, Miss Pia," Dasia said, her voice muffled as though she covered her mouth against the phone.

"How are you?"

"Did you find me a new home?" she asked rather than answer my question.

"Not yet," I hated to admit, my heart breaking anew. "But I've got something in the works—I should have an answer for you by Friday, okay? Can you hang in there for a few more days?"

Dasia let out a heavy breath. "I can't stand it here," she whispered. "He tried my door knob again last night."

Anger flared to life inside me, and I envisioned ripping Mr. Griffey's hands off his arms. Punching him right in the nose.

"I just avoid him as much as possible," Dasia said.

"Stick to his wife's side," I said. "Stay alert and make sure you don't end up alone with him—even for five minutes, alright?"

"Yeah. I'm trying."

"You'll be eighteen in a couple of months, Dasia. Then you'll have your freedom. Promise."

———

Dasia called me from her friend's cell phone late the next morning while I sat in traffic trying to get to the office after working from home for a few hours.

"Dasia?" I asked in answer, having saved her friend's number and answering the call regardless of the new hands-free law.

She sobbed, and my heart stalled out.

I clutched my steering wheel tighter with my free hand. "Dasia! What happened?"

"Mrs. Griffey went to the gym before he left for work this morning," she sputtered between sobs, and I grit my teeth, beyond angry—beyond hurt for the poor girl.

"What did he do?"

"Cornered me. Grabbed my breast." She sobbed again. "He tried to kiss me, but I kneed him in the balls."

"Good for you!"

"I-I took off. Ran all the way over to Stacey's—barefoot and in my PJs."

"Did you call the cops?"

"You know I can't do that!"

I wanted to curse her out like Ryker, telling her the fuck she couldn't.

"He's a somebody, Miss Pia. I'm a nobody—that means no one will believe me."

We'd had the discussion before, and the truth of her words slayed me to the point curse words rang inside my head on repeat.

"You stay with Stacey today, tonight if you can—I know where you are, so I'll find a way to get you out of the Griffey's right away."

*There has to be a way...*

Dasia sniffled in my ear. "Okay."

"Does Stacey know?"

"Yes."

"Her parents?"

"No."

Friends of the Griffey's, I doubted they would believe her anyway.

"You just stay there, you hear me?" I said, finally putting the car into drive as the cars ahead of me shifted forward.

"Okay."

"Call me if you need me."

Seconds later, I hung up and flung my cell over to the passenger seat, spouting off every swear word I knew until I sat fuming in silence, once more at a standstill in traffic as an ambulance sped by in the breakdown lane. Imagining what Dasia had gone through at that bastard's sick hands turned my stomach, and tears pricked my eyes.

My cell rang again, and I sprawled over the console, grasping for the phone just beyond reach. "Damnit!" Since I popped my car into park while waiting for the accident ahead to clear, I unhooked my seat belt and scooted close enough to grab it.

*Ryker.*

A sob caught in my throat at the sudden onslaught of emotion. "Hey," I managed to hold it together, forcing a smile so he wouldn't hear the tears in my voice. "How are you doing? How's Jenny?"

"What's wrong?" he asked without answering my questions, his tone wary and on alert even through the line.

I closed my eyes and inhaled deeply, knowing he wouldn't let it go. "Dasia's foster father sexually assaulted her."

"Where is she?" The question came out low. Deadly.

Shivers licked at my spine. "Safe at a friend's."

"Where are *you*?"

I opened my eyes, my shoulders slumped at the weight of feeling completely powerless. "Sitting in traffic."

"Did he fucking rape her?" Ryker asked, his tone

hinting at barely suppressed rage—understandably so.

"No," I whispered, horrified of the thought if she hadn't hit him in the nuts that he very well may have stolen her innocence.

"You need to get her the hell outta there."

"I can't." I bit back a sob. "Not legally, anyway, since she refuses to go to the authorities."

"Goddamn mother fucking…"

I swiped tears from my cheeks. "I think I've found a new home for her, but I won't know for sure until Friday."

"Friday might be too late," he snapped, and I choked on another sob knowing I might fail her further. "Are you okay?" he asked with less venom in his tone.

"I could really use a hug," I whispered my longing, sending an ache through my chest as tears coursed down my face.

"I'm sorry I can't be that for you, Pia."

"Yeah." I swallowed against my pain, my tumbling emotions, and the cars ahead of me finally started moving again. "I have to go," I whispered.

"Keep in touch, Pia. Let me know what happens, and maybe you and I can head out on the bike this weekend."

Something to smile about—but my lips didn't even twitch. "I'd like that," I managed to choke out.

"Saturday?"

I would have Dasia placed elsewhere by then and would hopefully be able to enjoy a day away from reality. "Say the time and I'll be ready."

"I'll pick you up at nine—and Pia?"

"Yeah?"

"Pack an overnight bag."

Hope bubbled up enough to make my worry for Dasia bearable.

## RYKER

I'd spent an hour in the chop shop before caving and telling my chicken shit self to grow some goddamn balls and call Pia. Thank fuck I did.

I hung up and it took me all of two minutes to get a plan set in my head, before I headed out of the office to set it in motion. I grabbed a set of keys to one of the vehicles Sully, my other head mechanic, had readied to strip down, and checked to make sure it still had a set of stolen plates on the front and back of the car.

"Borrowing this one!" I hollered across the shop. "Lights all working?"

Sully glanced up from the engine he'd been bent over, ratchet in hand, giving the car I stood beside a quick once-over. "It's ready to roll. If you're goin' for lunch, grab me a sub, too!"

"Not coming back today—you're in charge."

"Ooo!" He chuckled and wiped his elbow across his scruffy cheek. "Hot date?"

"Fuck off!"

He lifted a greasy hand in a saluted wave and grinned, same as always when I took off from the shop. "Take it easy, boss!"

Easy.

I considered the word while speeding back home to change. Devil had given me all the shit on one Ted Griffey, billionaire CEO with the perfectly groomed hair and brilliant white smile.

Fucking sleaze ball. Cocksucking bastard.

While Vigil would have preferred I take a brother or three along with me to watch my back while I took care of business, I didn't have the time or patience to wait. The lust for blood, the rage to destroy, motored my mind forward as fast as the Screamin' Eagle I wished to have between my legs, rather than a stolen fucking car that brought on claustrophobia.

I put down the windows and managed to relax the slightest bit with the blast of fresh, hot air.

The fucker worked in downtown Boston, so I

knew I couldn't go rumbling in on my bike in leathers and a cut claiming me as a Vicious Viper. Stolen car, stolen plates, and jeans and a black t-shirt along with a ball cap it had to be.

A quick change out of my leathers at home, and I hopped back in the car, heading for Boston.

I dialed up Devil en route, not giving two fucks about the hands-free law and just staying alert for any fuzz hanging out ahead of me.

"Whatcha got, Ryker?" he answered.

"Need to know where that Griffey fuck is."

"What happened?"

"He went after the girl, but she escaped before he stuck his dick where it doesn't belong."

"Thank fuck for that," he muttered. "Give me a few—I'll get back to you."

I stared at the open highway, keeping the speed to five over the limit, the silence stifling. Tunnel-visioned by blood lust, I waited. My stomach hard, my jaw aching.

Took twenty minutes for Devil to call me back.

"He's in his office, and I've got the building's security system and the parking garages ready to shut down."

"I'm good to roll?"

"Have at the fucker, and give him a boot for me, too, will ya?"

Devil hated abuse just as much as I did—but for different reasons. He'd had his own innocence stolen by a priest, and the fucker claimed it's what twisted his mind.

I didn't consider him as sick in the head as me, but the club whores whispered about his liking of kinky shit. Whatever floated his boat—as long as it was consensual and no one got hurt without wanting it, I didn't give a shit what the fuck he did behind closed doors.

Two blocks and just over an hour to Griffey's usual quitting time, I told Devil to shut the system down. Whether he knocked out the feeds, put something on repeat, or some other sneaky shit, I didn't care. All I knew, is I could trust my brother to protect my ass from getting my face caught on camera anywhere near Griffey.

I parked in the parking garage he used, backed in and facing his BMW with its vanity plate about some "makin'it" shit. He might be making it big in the corporate world, but the rich CEO was about to have his ass handed to him, bar room brawl style.

Thoughts flooded my head while I waited, all

bringing an onslaught of emotion I couldn't fucking deal with.

Jenny had packed up Mom's shit and had picked up her ashes. I hated that I hadn't been able to offer physical comfort, same as I couldn't do for Pia. She captured my focus for a time, and I replayed our time together, how easy it was to talk to her—just fucking *be* with her.

I fucking missed her. Her smile and laughter, her sweet, fruity scent. My mind went to her body, her curves, and I flexed my fingers as they itched to touch—caress and give affection I craved myself.

I managed to lose myself in the fantasy to pass the time, even getting a semi. Griffey made an appearance, shutting all thoughts of Pia and my dick straight the fuck down, stirring my rage again. A leggy woman in a business suit chatted with him as they walked toward me.

"Fuck." I had no intention of hurting a woman, and the second she angled off down another row of cars, I breathed easier.

I hopped out of the car, shoulders hunched, trying to look less a threat than I was while checking out the immediate area. The woman pulled out of her parking spot on the other side of the garage and headed out—away from us.

Griffey strode toward his car, his focus on the cell in his hand, a briefcase-type bag occupying his other hand.

My heart rate slowed as I focused on even breathing—but rage spurred me onward, and I slowed a bit, judging distance ... keeping my foot falls quiet.

Out for a stroll in a goddamn parking garage like I had nothing better to do...

Griffey slid his cell into his suit coat, pulled out a set of keys, and hit the unlock. The BMW beeped.

Ten feet.

He glanced at me and nodded as I feigned a pathway behind him.

I dipped my head in response and turned my attention on the exit, keeping watch over him in my periphery.

Five feet.

He focused on his driver door, hand reaching out for the handle—and I dove at him in a burst of adrenaline, grasping his hair and smashing his face into the window.

"Ah!" He grunted as I smashed his face in a second time, kneeing up between his thighs at the same time. Another grunt ripped from him, and I let him go, stepping back, and glancing around as he crumpled to the ground.

Not a soul had witness the attack that I could see.

I crouched beside him, checking out my work. He clutched his bloody nose with one hand and his balls with the other while whimpering and curling into a ball. A fucking puddle of piss leaked onto the ground beneath his ass.

"D-don't hurt me ... cash in wallet." He coughed and moaned, writhing in pain, eyelids clenched shut. "Take it all—anything. J-just please leave me alone."

*Cocksucking pansy ass.*

I wondered if he even considered Dasia's pleas for him to stop before deciding to ignore them.

"You fucking touch your foster kid again, and I'll saw my blade across your throat," I whispered harshly while watching the blood dribble through his fingers covering his nose. "I've got eyes on you, Griffey," I growled the words. "Even in your own fucking home. Fuck up again, and I'll feed you to the fucking fish. Understand?"

He whimpered again and nodded.

"Words, cocksucker."

"Yes," he gasped out.

I stood, slammed my steel-tipped boot into his

kidney for Devil, and left the pussy lying there in his own piss and blood.

He hadn't moved by the time I got back to the car and pulled out. The adrenaline crash hit me quicker than usual, and my fingers shook as I dialed Devil. "It's done."

I hung up without another word, knowing my brother would do whatever necessary to undo what he'd done to watch my back. I clutched the steering wheel to keep my hands from shaking from the adrenaline crash after affects.

I turned north, intent on returning the car back to the chop shop and burning my clothes. The need for drinking a fifth of JD flitted through my brain, but I shut it down, even though I really wanted to go find Pia just to see her face from a distance. Drink *her* the fuck down instead.

14

───────

**PIA**

The new foster family for Dasia fell through.

I sat and stared at the phone I'd hung up after hearing the terrible news. With no other home to place her in, Dasia had no choice but to return to the Griffey's. That, or run away again and live on the streets, which I couldn't stomach the thought of. I'd never known such disappointment, not even when losing who'd I'd hoped would be *my* forever family when I'd been a young teenage girl.

Heaving a heavy sigh didn't help as I reached for my cell, needing to call her.

Stacey answered—and told me that her parents had sent Dasia home earlier that morning.

"Can I ask why?" I prodded, curious if she'd been

talking about Mr. Griffey and pissed Stacey's parents off.

"You didn't hear?" Stacey asked, her voice raising like a typical teenage girl sharing the latest drama and gossip. "Mr. Griffey got mugged after leaving work last night!"

"What?"

"Yeah, he left the office and someone beat him up. Took off with his wallet and briefcase."

"Is he alright?" Not that I *truly* cared...

"He had to get stitches. Broken nose or something my mom said. Personally," her voice lowered to a whisper, "I'm thinking karma is paying him back for what he did to Dasia."

I wanted to agree, but couldn't discuss those types of things with Dasia's friend. After thanking her for the information, I hung up—and immediately dialed the Griffey's house number.

Mrs. Griffey answered and repeated what Stacey had told me, assuring me her husband was fine, again not that I cared, before handing the phone over to Dasia.

"Can you hold on a sec?" Dasia asked, then I heard her muffled voice tell Mrs. Griffey she was taking the phone to her room if that was alright.

A minute later, a door closed.

"You'll never guess what happened!" she holler-whispered in my ear.

"I heard Mr. Griffey got mugged last night."

"Well, that, too, but he apologized to me," Dasia said. "When I got back here this morning, he was sitting in the living room with an ice pack on his face. You should see him—busted nose, stitches, black eyes." She laughed quietly. "Totally got the shit kicked out of him!"

"What do you mean he apologized?" I asked rather than laugh along with her like I really wanted to do.

"Oh. Yeah." Muffled shifting sounded in my ear. "When his wife left the living room," Dasia whispered again, "he stared right at me—but not creepy at all—and said he'd made a mistake, that he would take it back if he could. Said it wouldn't happen again, that he'd had a moment of weakness. Stress at work and that sort of shit."

"Huh." I wasn't sure *what* to make of the apology.

"Right?"

"So how do you feel about the situation?"

"Not as bad as I did yesterday," Dasia said, and I could hear an ease in her voice I hadn't for months. "The guy is still an ass for what he did, though."

I exhaled another heavy breath. "Well, I have some bad news."

"I have to stay here, don't I?" The disappointment in her voice stung.

"Yes. I'm sorry, Dasia. The foster home I'd hoped to place you in isn't going to work out."

"Well, that sucks ass."

"I'm sorry," I repeated, my own disappointment rising again. "But it sounds like things might be okay."

"Dunno. Seems to be, but I've only been back for like two hours."

While I appreciated Mr. Griffey's recognizing he'd done wrong and apologizing for it, a nagging feeling in my gut made me not trust him. I didn't want to upset or worry Dasia, but I reminded her to still be careful and left it at that. I also promised to continue looking for something else.

Feeling somewhat relieved, but not entirely as I would have been placing Dasia elsewhere, I told myself I would hope for the best and try to enjoy my weekend away.

Butterflies danced in my belly the rest of the day, and sleep didn't come easily that night.

Saturday morning, I checked in with Dasia—no change, and her foster father made no attempts on her doorknob during the night. That bubbling hope returned in full force after hanging up, and I showered and shaved, mentally preparing myself for a nice long ride on the back of Ryker's motorcycle and the sure, sore backside in exchange for another taste of freedom.

He'd said to pack an overnight bag, so I dug out an old backpack, thinking that would be the best since bikes didn't have real back seats or trunks.

Ryker surprised me by knocking on my door a half hour early, but I'd been ready and waiting, jitters keeping me from sitting down to wait patiently. Black leather pants clung to his thighs, and another white t-shirt did the same to his chest I couldn't wait for another peek of. Damn, I wished I could touch...

Warmth slid up over me to my cheeks as a corner of his lips twitched and he shut the door behind him. "Looking good, little lamb."

A rush of arousal slicked the sexy panties I'd bought for our outing even though knowing the thong would drive me insane on the bike.

His focus settled on my chest, and my nipples pebbled beneath his stare. Did he want to touch? Nibble? More of those bubbles sprang up inside me, and I decided to push just a bit. I lifted my girls, helping them spill halfway out of the top of my shirt.

"Want a taste?" I whispered, all breathy with lust.

He raised an eyebrow while lifting his focus to my face, his hands fisted at his sides. "Did you pack a bag?" he asked instead, all the wind leaking from my randy sails.

"Yeah." I dropped the girls and turned to grab my backpack off the couch, bending over the back like I'd done the weekend before. Didn't hurt to try, right?

Ryker groaned, and I wiggled my backside while glancing over my shoulder. "That offer of a taste still stands..."

"Goddamnit, woman." He didn't move.

*Fine. The day is young.*

I laughed and turned, slipping my bag onto my back. "I'm ready to roll if you are."

Shaking his head, Ryker led the way out of my apartment. The second surprise came when he stopped alongside a different Harley—an actual two-seater with saddle bags.

He unbuckled the one on the right and motioned me to stuff my backpack inside. I did and buckled it back up while eyeing my new seat. It looked ten times more comfy than the one that had numbed my ass—but I wouldn't have to hold onto his cut or touch his thighs while pretending to hold on tighter, either.

"How many bikes do you have?" I asked while buckling on the helmet he handed to me.

"Only the one."

"Whose is this?"

"Warden's. He's an enforcer. Got himself an old lady and decided he needed a second seat."

"Smart man." I grinned and climbed aboard as he started the engine. The pipes on Warden's bike weren't as loud as Ryker's, but the rush of wind, the exhilaration of speeding along the highway with whipping wind around me felt the same.

I laughed, closed my eyes, tipped my head back, and just enjoyed the hell out of life.

———

Ryker had gotten us a room in Ogunquit—with a king-sized bed rather than two doubles, which thrilled me to *death*. I'd get another chance to maybe wake up somehow entwined with his hard muscles and warm skin.

The thought kept me in a constant state of arousal, even while hanging out on the beach, enjoying the cooler breeze blowing in off the ocean. Even had I known we headed to the beach, I wouldn't have opted for a bathing suit. My girls and bits of spandex did not get along enough for my liking.

For forty-three, Ryker rocked his trunks, and I couldn't keep my eyes off him as he dove into the waves and came up dripping, water running in rivulets down his shaved head and beard. He smiled—a full-on grin like a kid before diving in a second time.

"Get your ass out here!" he called to me.

How could I resist?

Soaked panties and shorts, soaked bra and tank top, but I joined him, wetting my own hair that had been flattened by the helmet anyway. The makeup I'd painted on my face melted away in the salt water—but I hadn't even thought of it until Ryker smirked while looking at my face.

"Drowned rat?" I asked, not offended in the least as he chuckled.

"Black-eyed rat."

I splashed water at him. "Bastard."

He chuckled, and a wave slammed into us, tugging me downward.

I shrieked and reached out on instinct, grabbing

hold of his arm to keep me above water. Finding my feet, I balanced—and realized his hand held my hip.

Heat rushed through me as I blinked the water from my eyes and peered up at him. Less than a foot of space separating us. A smaller wave rocked the water, merely swaying us on our feet—but he stepped back as though I'd burned him, twisting his arm to rid him of my hold.

"Sorry," I murmured, my heart squeezing in my chest.

His beard twitched as though he clenched his jaw, and he nodded. "I'm fucking starved."

I smiled brightly, fake as hell, and nodded. "Food sounds good."

I swallowed against the disappointment popping those hopeful bubbles, and followed him out of the water. He had reached out to steady me on my feet— a protective nature to override his wound or fear.

We still had the night and next day. I hung my hat on the progress made and the determination to continue down that path.

## 15

## RYKER

My hand had shot out on its own to steady Pia—and fear had ripped me away. But I couldn't keep from looking at her lips the rest of the day. She'd been so close, so vulnerable in her gaze, the desire in her eyes while peering up at me in the ocean ... I'd almost given into the need to pull her close against my chest.

Couldn't fucking do it.

I stared at her lips while we ate lunch at a clam shack, our clothes still damp in some spots, rigid from salt water in others. A real date, her sandals sometimes brushing against my feet beneath the picnic table and all.

Her mouth. Pouty. Full lips. Every swipe of her

tongue over their pinkness sent an ache through my balls.

I couldn't kiss them, but I sure as fuck could have them wrapped around my dick.

We returned to the hotel room after another hour on the beach eating ice cream cones—another blue ball punch to my groin with every dart of her tongue. She insisted I shower first since she would take longer, and the second I exited the bathroom, a towel wrapped around my waist, she looked up from her cell, her gaze snagging on me.

"Damn," she whispered, tossing her cell aside.

I stepped out of her way as she approached with her bag in hand even though I'd have preferred grabbing her and tossing her ass on the bed for me to devour, saltiness from the ocean on her skin be damned.

My fucking hands shook with the need to do it. Dick swelled. Mouth salivated like a goddamn drooling dog.

The bathroom door clicked behind her, and I closed my eyes, letting out a slow exhale.

Fuck, how I wished I could tear down the goddamn walls inside me. Wished like hell overcoming the stress of my childhood came easy. I had the perfect opportunity, the perfect woman—kind, nurturing, and sweet—but the goddamn fear...

Scowling, I tossed the towel onto the room's chair and sat, legs spread, dick at half-mast.

I listened to the shower run, imagining Pia running her hands over her body, every swell, dip, and curve. Until the water shut off, my balls seized up, my dick leaked, and I worked my hand up and down with slow strokes.

Waiting.

The door creaked open, and Pia pulled up abruptly in the doorway as her gaze landed on me. Damp blonde hair hung around her beautiful makeup-less face, and a see through t-shirt covered her from chest to thigh, but I couldn't keep my focus off her mouth.

"Come here, little lamb." I growled the command.

She caught her lower lip between her teeth, but didn't hesitate to close the distance between us and kneel without being asked. The scent of juicy watermelon swarmed over me as she gave me that same fucking look she had in the ocean. All lust and need.

"Want a taste?" I asked, my voice rugged as I pushed against the base of my dick to offer it to her.

Her goddamn dimple popped as she smiled,

entwining her hands behind her back without being asked. "Please."

*Goddamn...*

The warmth of her mouth closed over me, and I groaned while watching my length disappear until she gagged.

"Only take what you can," I told her—and found my fingers wrapping in her hair without thought.

*Fuck.*

But I couldn't let go. She moaned and lowered her face once more, my being in a seated position making her forehead brush my abs, her shoulders against the insides of my thighs.

I felt like a goddamn engine ready to combust—fire and fuel mixing to the point I went light headed with every swipe of her tongue, every gentle scrape of her teeth.

My fingers tightened in her hair, and I pulled her back with a pop. "On the bed." Fuck, I didn't sound like me—raspy as hell, uneven tone, fucking shaking voice.

She rocked back onto her heels and up to her feet the second I released her. "How do you want me, Ryker?" she asked with a whisper, her voice all sexy and low.

*Any way. Every goddamn way. Face to face—wrapped up in your softness.*

"On your knees. Ass up."

Pia pulled her shirt up over her head leaving her naked from perfect tits to unpainted perfect pinky toe, and I drank my fill while grasping the base of my dick to keep from shooting spunk up over my chest.

She crawled onto the bed, her lush ass swaying, tantalizing...

"Closer to the headboard," I said, standing. "Keep your legs together."

Pia bent forward, chest to the bed and ass in the air, the top of her head against the headboard. Wetness smeared at the junction of her thighs, but the holes I wanted to claim couldn't be seen with her legs pressed tightly together.

I grabbed a condom from my bag and rolled it on while climbing onto the bed behind her.

"Fuck, you've got curves to drive a man mad," I growled, straddling her legs, dick in hand. One swipe of my sheathed dick up through her crack coated me with creaminess my mouth drooled for.

I'd never tasted a woman in my life. Not fucking once.

I ran the pad of my thumb over the tip of the

condom and lifted it to my nose. Musky and sweet. My goddamn taste buds *ached.*

I licked, and the tanginess of her filled my mouth, jerking my dick against her ass. The desire to shove my face in her pussy and devour every inch of her slammed into me, stealing my breath.

I shoved balls deep into her body without warning to keep from crossing that hard line.

She shrieked and grasped the pillow beneath her head while I grabbed hold of the headboard and plowed into her over and over. Lost. Fucking gone on her scent, her taste. Over-fucking-whelmed like an animal hell bent on tearing her in two.

Pia fucking consumed me—every goddamn thought, every emotion—if only she could consume the walls inside me with the same fire ignited through my body.

I wanted to let loose the cum boiling in my balls, but I needed more.

Had to fucking have it.

I pulled back onto my heels. "Roll over."

Her chest heaved as she peered up at me, her tits swayed off to her side, nipples hardened points. Pupils blown fucking wide open ... her lips parted with pants.

"Grab the headboard."

She obeyed.

"Feet on the mattress—spread your thighs for me just like last time, little lamb." My voice shook— her entire body shook.

Her pussy lips, puffed and glistening set the water works in my mouth on full onslaught, but I lifted my focus to her face.

More.

I crowded in close, my dick finding home, my thighs against her spread ones, my hands inches from hers on the headboard—my focus on her eyes.

Goddamn it all to fucking hell—she owned me.

I dragged out of her pussy, holding her gaze, drinking in every shift of emotion in her light eyes same as the first time I'd fucked her face to face.

"Ryker," she whisper-moaned my name, lifting her hips to meet me as I dipped into her again.

Pink crept up her chest, coated her cheeks as I slowly fucked in and out of her, barely holding onto my sanity. Every flex of my ass buried my dick inside her warmth. Every grind of my pelvis against her clit pulled a gasp from her parted lips.

I wanted to taste. Eat. Lick and bite.

A haze over-shadowed her eyes as they widened.

"Oh..." She arched beneath me, her tits brushing me—but the clench of her sweet pussy around my aching length overrode the skin on skin contact of our chests. The intense energy, the emotion radiating from her eyes pulled me under.

My balls fucking exploded, and I grunted, slamming into her body's grasp, shot after shot of cum seeming to rip from my groin with a pain so goddamn sweet, I didn't want it to end. Couldn't fucking look away from her face. Flushed. Beautiful.

One last shudder ripped through me, slamming my eyes shut.

Head hanging, hands in a death grip on the headboard, I stilled, buried inside her, groin still flush against the slick silk of hers. Unable to move.

She touched my beard, and I reared back on instinct, slipping from her body.

"Fuck."

"Sorry," she hastened to say, pushing up to her elbows. "I didn't mean—"

"It's okay." I scrubbed a hand down over my face, trying to still the slamming of my heart her touch had activated. "I'm sorry. Fuck. Sorry, Pia."

I rolled off the bed and escaped into the bathroom, eyeing myself in the mirror—cursing myself while rolling off the condom and tying it up.

*Fucking loser. Pathetic fuck can't even stand a woman's light touch on your beard for fuck's sake.*

I threw the condom in the trash, scowling and teeth grit, while getting a warm, wet towel for Pia.

She didn't utter a word when I took it to her, nor when I sat on the edge of the bed, elbows on knees, and face in my hands.

"I'm sorry," I repeated.

"Am I the only woman you've had sex with like that?"

I lifted up and turned to find her on her side, hands tucked beneath her cheek.

It would be so easy to drown in her eyes...

"Yes," I rasped.

Her smile warmed up the coldness inside me. "Thank you for sharing that part of you with me."

My eyes stung. Fucking *stung*.

Klingon's words decided to ring in my ears, and I twisted toward her.

"Touch my beard, Pia."

Her breath caught, and she peered up at me, silent.

"Please," I said. "You caught me off guard—but I want you to. Try. Please."

She slowly sat, her attention not leaving my face.

I tensed as her hand lifted, but focused on her eyes, the desire pouring from them. My breath caught at the first, gentle brush.

*Don't. Fucking. Move.*

Stone cold, unmoving, I endured her fingers on my beard, my gut clenching even though my dick stirred to life again.

Pia's hand dropped to her lap, her eyes shining with tears—but smiling. Goddamn, did she smile. "Thank you," she whispered again, and I found myself falling even harder, something I didn't think possible.

Sudden fear snaked in like a goddamn thief, and I moved away, intent on my leathers and bike. "Want to ride?"

"Definitely."

Fifteen minutes later, we shot up Route 1, but I didn't shy away from the brush of her thighs— fucking craved the motion with an ache almost as painful as the truth I could never be what she needed.

## 16

## PIA

My ass was worn out. Exhausted. Sunburned from nose to toes by the time Ryker dropped me off at my apartment Sunday night. He didn't take me up on the offer to stay, but I didn't push.

Waking up face to face—but not touching—had still satisfied in some way. He hadn't asked me to touch him again, and I made sure to hold myself in check, but the hope inside me couldn't be defeated.

We'd gone out for a real dinner twice. We'd made love face to face again—I couldn't call what we'd done fucking. The emotional connection we had went beyond anything I'd experienced, hell, beyond anything I'd hoped for, and I found contentment in that even though I hadn't yet tasted his lips.

Yet.

He spent the week up north at his home, his club, while I toiled away still trying to find my missing girl and find Dasia a new home. The high of the weekend diminished with each passing day as dreariness crept in with the constant clouds and drizzle.

At least the heat wave ended. I had a sweater wrapped around me beneath the umbrella while running into Dunks Tuesday morning. Jesse handed me my coffee—and two donuts in a bag because I deserved them, damnit.

Ryker liked my thighs, anyway.

Jesse hadn't heard a peep about Sophia, and when he'd asked, I assured him Dasia was doing better.

Griffey watched her enough to creep her out, but he kept his hands to himself and hadn't tried any funny stuff. I told her I was still searching for a new home for her.

Tuesday night over the phone, Ryker's rumbling voice and commands had my fingers buried inside my pussy—and I came hard, his name on my lips, my life a bit brighter again.

Wednesday night it poured, and I watched him

on video chat jerk himself off, his curses and grunts making me as wet as the stoop of my apartment.

"I want to watch you, little lamb," he said when he finished. "Put your fingers inside that sweet pussy—let me see."

His groaned words sent another rush of wetness to drip from my core, and I held my cell down *there*—not even ashamed or embarrassed by the wet noises my fingers made sliding in and out of my needy channel.

"Come for me, Pia," he growled. "Soak your fingers."

I did.

"Be a filthy little lamb and lick them clean. Tell me how sweet you taste."

Heat flooded my face on that command, but I did what he wanted, missing him and his loving so damn much I wanted to cry.

I hoped for another weekend together, but he called Thursday and said the club had things going on.

I resigned myself to a quiet weekend at home, something I hadn't had for a while—and did not enjoy.

Books, wine, ice cream—silence of the good kind

from the Dasia and Griffey asshole front—I should have been in heaven.

My thoughts on heaven had changed, or rather, Ryker had changed them for me. I missed his nearness, the scent of his soap, his voice, his scowl, even.

He promised the following weekend—and I hung my hat and hopes on that invitation.

Friday morning, I grabbed my mail from the previous couple of days while slugging down my first cup of coffee. The cool morning air filled my lungs, waking me more than the damn caffeine. Birds tweeted their happiness at the rising sun, but I scowled.

Amid the pile of junk and bills was a card with my name and address perfectly printed on the front—handwriting I recognized.

*Fucking Martínez.*

I tossed aside the mail and set my coffee down before ripping the envelope open. Not bothering to read the fancy script, I scanned to the bottom of the card, affirming what I'd guessed.

Martínez didn't give two shits about my mom—

he'd told me in Dunks he'd heard she wasn't doing well and hadn't inquired over her health or the stage four lung cancer she'd been diagnosed with a couple months earlier. No, the fucker sent that card to let me know he had eyes and ears about. We hadn't published an obituary, and Jenny only let those who'd been close with mom know she'd passed.

And the fact he'd sent the card to my home in Topsfield rather than Mom's condo where I'd been staying? He wanted me to know he was watching, that nothing escaped his notice.

I tossed the card aside and scrubbed a hand down over my scruffy scalp.

A quick call through to Klingon eased the anxiety twisting my gut a bit, but sure as fuck didn't ease my mind.

The Vipers headed up to Maine that night for the weekend. Warden's old lady, Shaun, had purchased twenty acres of wilderness earlier in the summer, and the contractors she'd hired to set up a dozen rough-pine bunk houses had finally finished the job.

Over twenty bikes rumbled up 95, Scully following with a truck and trailer full of food, sleeping bags, grills, and other shit the old ladies had decided we need for our two night stay. We'd never made a full-on road trip, and the comradery made me want to smile. We'd been too busy packing up and readying to leave, that my brothers and their new lovers weren't all over each other, making me uncomfortable.

Longing for Pia had me scratching my chest on more than one occasion, and even though we'd had some hot as fuck phone sex—another first for my old ass—I hadn't invited her to come along.

She was too good for the likes of me, a cold hearted bastard who liked to bloody his hands alongside his Viper brothers, and she sure as fuck wouldn't fit in.

Two of said brothers got into a drunken fight Friday night not an hour after we set up camp in Maine. One lost a tooth, another ended up with a crooked nose. I'd let them have at it, even though as Sergeant at Arms, I shouldn't have. The fuckers had been toeing the line for months—nothing better than a bare knuckle brawl to settle the score of whatever bullshit rode them.

The fuckers even hugged afterward and clanked bottles of JD together before ambling off to get even more shit-faced than they already were.

I sat by the bonfire alongside Vigil, his brother Ricky, our VP, and Devil on my other side. The two of them bullshitted about pussy and getting their fucking fill, but I couldn't get my mind off Pia.

Soft, warm, little lamb, who listened so well when told to keep her hands put.

The fire crackled, sending a red ember onto my jeans. I flicked it off and swigged on my beer, leaning back in my folding chair to check out the vast expanse of stars overhead as the marijuana smoke from Vigil's joint drifted past me.

A radio played over near one of the bunk houses, and voices raised here and there—some laughing, some singing. Three of the old ladies and a couple of whores Vigil allowed to come along for the weekend danced beyond the fire, beer bottles in hand, cut off shorts and crop tops not even twitching my dick.

"Where the fuck you at, Ryker?"

I lifted my head back toward the stars, ignoring Vigil and his high as fuck ass.

"That woman?" he pushed.

"Yeah," I admitted, swigging on my beer again.

"Devil said you took care of that prick touching the kid she's in charge of."

I hadn't told Vigil about the mess and what I'd done to hopefully clean it up. Hadn't involved the club, so I'd kept the shit to myself. The less who knew, the better. Devil must have been the one to blab, the loose-tongued fuck.

"I did," I told Vigil, turning toward him, ready to take whatever shit he tossed my way.

He peered at me while sucking on his joint, one side of his face hid in darkness, the other pale eye and bushy brow lit by the flickering flames beside us. "Shit like that comes up again, you tell me," he said while fighting to hold the smoke in his lungs. "Let your brothers have your back."

I nodded, knowing that's exactly what he'd have wanted.

He let the cloud escape his lips. "I know it's personal for you."

Another swallow of beer slid down my throat.

"But that makes it personal for all of us. Understand?"

I nodded again.

"When are you going to bring her around?"

I shook my head, eyeing the burning joint in his hand.

"Broody bastard."

"Takes one to know one," I tossed out.

"Why didn't you invite her this weekend? You're obviously fucking gone on her—glazed eyes and all that shit like you're dreaming of flowering fields and picket fences."

I scowled, suddenly not having as much fun as I'd been having. "The fuck I do."

He snorted a laugh, more a goddamn giggle thanks to the pot. "She's got you wrapped around her goddamn little finger if you ask me."

"Not asking you," I grunted the words. "Besides, she's too good for all of this." I swept my hand out, indicating the whole fucking camp. Pot heads. Drunks. Whores sucking off brothers at the camp's edge. Dozens of hands that had been bloodied by violence. "She doesn't belong here."

"Like Warden's heiress?" Vigil asked with a snort before filling his lungs again. The seconds ticked by while he held the smoke in his lungs. "Or Stone's successful model—the judge's daughter who's dancing over there and living it up?" he asked with a steady exhale of smoke.

"You know what I mean," I said through grit teeth.

"No, I don't. Pia is a social worker—hard-working blue collar, same as most of your brothers and their old ladies who work outside the home."

I cast him a side-eye, my gaze narrowed. "How the fuck you know so much about her?"

"I make it a point to know who is fucking with my brothers." He offered me the joint, but I shook my head. "Make it a point to watch over every single one of your asses—even if you don't think you need looking after."

He sucked down another hit, the glowing ember close to his fingers, and unsure what to say, I didn't bother opening my fucking mouth.

Giada abandoned the dancing women and slid onto Stone's lap, their mouths fusing, his hand finding her ass.

I looked away.

"You let her touch you yet?" Vigil asked, flicking what was left of his burned out joint into the fire.

I drank down the last of my beer while recalling her touch on my beard—the only one I'd allowed the rest of that weekend we'd spent in Ogunquit. "Not much more than I let the club whores."

"Why the fuck not?"

I turned to fully face Vigil—one of my best friends. "I want it. Fucking crave it like a goddamn lunatic," I spewed the shit from my aching chest.

"So what's the problem?"

"You know what my fucking problem is," I said, keeping my voice low even though Devil and Ricky laughed in their own little world of pussy and tit stories on my other side. "You're one of the few who does."

"What's Klingon say?"

He *would* know I'd go to my childhood friend first. "To take baby steps."

"So you're at least trying?"

"Trying."

Vigil leaned over to grab a bag of chips off the ground beside him. He offered the opened end toward me.

"I'm good."

"Anything new on that shit show over Stone's woman?" Vigil asked loudly, definitely intending for the other officers around the fire to hear.

The question caught Devil's attention who leaned forward, elbows on knees. "Your buddy Martínez is down in South America," he told me.

"And Klingon says all is quiet in Vegas," I added, letting the others know what I'd already told Vigil.

"And my sister says our father hasn't even mentioned the Vipers," Giada pipped up from across the fire.

"I'm not afraid of that fat fuck," Vigil said around a mouthful of chips.

"Might want to be if he gets elected to the Senate in a few months," Ricky muttered.

"Tell them about the card," Vigil changed the conversation before cramming another handful of chips into his mouth.

"Martínez send me a condolence card."

"Nice of him," Ricky grunted while staring into the fire.

"Fucker didn't give two shits about her," I tossed at him, my tone sharp as my glare on his face. "Didn't even ask about her when I'd met him that morning at Dunks."

"Fucking prick," Devil said, crossing his arms. "Thought you two grew up together."

"We did, but he's a selfish, arrogant cocksucker." I sat back, gaze scanning around the campfire and the other officers. Even though Giada and Shaun had joined us, Vigil had told me to share the club business. Guess that meant all of it.

"Worse part," I said, rubbing a hand over my scalp, "is he knew to send the card to my house rather than Mom's condo where I'd been staying. He knew I'd left Southie and wanted me to know he knew it."

"Sure he wasn't just reaching out as an old friend?"

"We didn't put an obituary in the paper," I told Ricky who peered at me, his pale eyes glinting in the firelight. "And she only had a couple of friends Jenny called after she'd passed. She wasn't a known woman around Southie, so how would he have known about her death unless he's been watching me—my family?"

"Fuck," Warden cursed, shifting Shaun on his lap. "Think Jenny needs someone watching her back?"

"She's in Vegas. Suppose I could give Klingon a call." I scratched at my chest. "Vigil?"

He shrugged, his pot-reddened eyes peering at me while he crunched on another mouthful of chips.

"Warden?" I asked, turning once more to the man who would think about my family's security. His company had been getting paid to watch people's asses for years.

"Your call, Ryker, but if I had a sister…"

"Call him," Stone said, his cool gaze catching mine through the fire. As Warden's number one employee, he'd think that way, too.

"Think the situation warrants that kind of heightened security?" I asked, glancing around again at all my brothers. "She's so fucking far away, and the one's he'll want if he finds out anything—us—are all right here. Our fucking families are all right here."

"Yeah," Warden said, "but we've got security already in place. Jenny's on her own."

"Better to be safe than sorry," Giada spoke up. "We took precautions and still lost my brother." Her voice choked up, and Stone tugged her closer. "You don't want to lose a sibling, Ryker," she whispered. "Trust me on that."

I held her intense stare above the flickering flames. She'd been to fucking hell and back—the woman knew pain.

"I'll call Klingon," I said.

A few of my brothers nodded.

"Fuck, this shit is a mood killer," Vigil muttered. "I need another joint. Or a whore."

"Please," Shaun said with an eye roll.

"All out of pot so I guess I'll just have to go get my dick sucked," Vigil said with a grin, grabbing between his spread legs, the high fucker.

Both Shaun and Giada made gagging noises, same as every time he made that statement in their presence.

"Everything is gonna be okay," Devil said to me as Vigil wondered away in search of a club whore whose mouth wasn't already full of Viper dick. "That shit got cleaned up. No fucking way Martínez will find a goddamn thing. I'm getting another beer," he said while pushing up. "You want one?"

I shook my head, telling myself that everything would be okay. Sure as fuck didn't feel like it though. He meandered off.

"I'll take one, you asshole!" Ricky hollered after him.

Stone and Giada went back to sucking face, and I had a sudden hankering for watermelon. My legs grew restless, my gaze flitting across the camp and the ruckus that had heightened around me while we'd been talking business. Rubbing at my forearm, I considered missing Pia was probably what set me on edge.

Or, maybe it was the memory of her touchy-feeling hands.

A shiver rippled over me as I moved my finger-tips from my forearm, but I couldn't decide if it was longing or loathing over the memory—the want—of her touch.

## 18

## PIA

I finally got a lead on Sophia while slaving away, stifled to death in my office on Monday morning.

A voice message on my extension at work—the young woman herself.

"Hey," the low, husky voice I would know anywhere. "Heard you were worrying about me—no need to. I'm making it just fine on my own. Take care, Miss Pia."

I sobbed. Literally shook in my chair, tears coursing down my cheeks as a weight I hadn't realized lay over me lifted fully.

Sophia was okay.

I wondered what had taken her so freaking long to call me and let me know, but maybe she hadn't known how upset I was over her disappearance. She didn't leave a number, but I could live with that.

She was alive. Sounded better than I'd ever heard her.

Moving onto the Dasia case blew the wind from my sails, though. Mr. Griffey started to creep her out again. Watched her. Brushed against her twice on Sunday—before muttering an apology.

I didn't trust the snake, not one bit.

I spent the next couple of days going through files, making phone calls, *begging* other families to make themselves available for a young woman a few months away from eighteen.

No one offered. I came up empty, feeling I failed the poor girl.

Wednesday afternoon, I sat, head in hands on my desk, my stomach unhappy as it had been since waking from a disturbing dream. I couldn't remember it clearly—didn't want to, but Dasia's tears, her sobs, remained in the forefront of my mind.

*Just a dream*, I told myself for at least the tenth time.

My cell rang, and I picked myself up off the desk, bleary-eyed and tired as hell thanks to the three a.m. jolt awake I hadn't been able to shake.

Ryker.

I smiled, my insides sighing as I swiped to answer. "Hey."

"I'm in town."

Blinking, I straightened in my chair. "Oh?"

"Want to go out for dinner?"

"Yes." I shut down the open tabs on my computer before he could say another word.

"What are you in the mood for?"

*You.*

"Did you bring the bike?" I asked instead.

"Yeah."

"Warden's comfy one or yours?"

"Mine—sorry."

I couldn't stop smiling. An excuse to push those touching boundaries, my ass be damned. "That's fine."

"I'll pick you up at six?"

"I'm leaving the office now," I said, glancing at the clock. Four. Too early, but I needed to breathe. I could feign sickness and take a few hours sick time. "We can go sooner if you want."

"A half-hour?"

"Sounds good."

I scurried to shut everything down for the day, telling myself I'd dive back into Dasia's case in the morning. Butterflies fluttering and insides jittering, I hurried back to my apartment, *so* ready to live again.

———

"You didn't answer my question," I said with a laugh, stirring my tonic with its straw.

Ryker peered across the table at me—a real dining table, at a steakhouse with dimmed lights and everything.

"Well?" I prompted, trying to bite back a smirk.

"Eleven."

"What?" I didn't mean to laugh, but I totally did, sitting back in my seat. "Eleven? I don't think I even knew what sex was at that age."

Ryker glanced around the dining room, and I swore a hint of pink flushed his cheeks.

"Who was it?"

"Some girl in the neighborhood. Older. Offered to take all three of our cherries."

I bit my lip, knowing my eyes danced. Sipping my drink, I watched his face, noticed his shift on the seat. He'd told me about the two boys he'd hung around with all throughout childhood until into their twenties when they went their separate ways.

"It was the first time I realized I could never be normal."

I sobered quick as hell. "She tried to touch you?"

He shook his head, pushing his empty plate away to cross his arms on the table without meeting my gaze. "I went last—saw the hickey on Martínez's neck when he came out, smug as a goddamn dog with a bone. The scratches on Klingon's cheek after his turn churned my stomach."

With a shrug, he finally lifted his focus to my face. "I knew right then I didn't want her hands on me. Couldn't be a chicken shit, though. I went in, told her to bend over the edge of her bed and not touch me or I'd to hurt her if she did—not in the good way I figured she'd like, either. Wasn't my best moment."

"My first was awful," I blurted, needing to take his mind off what should have been a good memory for him. "His ... thing was all of three inches."

"Dick. Say the word, Pia."

I swallowed, my face heating.

"Come on. You blurted all kinds of sewage that first day we met."

"Fine." I cleared my throat and straightened. "His dick wasn't much to look at, but at least it didn't hurt like I'd expected."

Ryker's eyes hardened. "How long were you with him before giving it up?"

"Six months. I was twenty-two."

One of his eyebrows shot upward. "Why the hell did you wait so damn long?"

I shrugged, glancing away. "Didn't exactly have anyone interested in popping mine, if you know what I mean."

"No. I don't know what you mean."

Anger furrowed his brow when I glanced back over at him. He studied my face. My neck, my chest —until the table blocked his downward appraisal. "You're fucking fine, Pia Hill. Fucking *fine*. I wish I was norm—"

He snapped his jaw shut, and I longed to reach over the table to touch his arm. "I think you're fucking fine just the way you are, too, Ryker McGrath," I whispered, leaning closer. "And if all I can have is a brush of clothing, or a three-second touch of my fingers to your beard, I'll be happy."

"You couldn't possibly."

"I think with time things could be different."

He eyed me for a while, the play of emotions on his face plain for me to inspect. Longing. Fear. Shutting down.

I forced a smile. "Ready to roll?" I asked, sitting

back and slipping on the light sweatshirt I'd needed since the all the rain had brought on a much cooler late August.

His lips didn't twitch. "Sure," he muttered, and tossed a few twenties on the table. "Let's ride."

## 19

## RYKER

The fuck was wrong with me? I wanted her touch. Wanted her arms wrapped around me while I sped back southward toward Boston. I wanted her cheek pressed against my cut, her hands creeping up under my shirt, warm palms on my abs.

My dick even jerked thinking about it. So, why the goddamn cold shiver down my spine?

She invited me in once we pulled up to her apartment. I followed her in like a lost dog, wanting to beg for scraps, beg for fucking affection I didn't know how to handle.

We went straight to the kitchen where she offered me a beer. Having no intention of staying the night, I turned the offer down.

She poured herself a glass of wine and ambled into the living room, me once more on her heels.

My throat felt tight as fuck, and I didn't know what to do with my hands.

Pia sat first—right in the middle of the goddamn couch, and I lowered myself down beside her, antsy and tense as fuck. Same as last time we'd sat on her couch, she angled toward me, drawing her knee up onto the cushion inches away from my thigh.

"How's Dasia?" I asked the first non-sexual, emotional thing to pop into my head.

She didn't answer right away, and I glanced over to find her peering at me with that stare, the one that saw too fucking deep. "Oh. My. God." She straightened, her hold on her wine glass tightening. "You did it, didn't you?"

"What?"

Her lips pursed for a second, and she set her wine onto the coffee table, putting a few more inches between us. "Don't *what* me, Ryker. You know exactly what I'm talking about! Ted Griffey!"

Her withdrawing tightened my gut more than the mention of his name. "What about him?"

"You put the fear of God into him."

"Yeah. So?"

"So?" Her eyes tried to bug out of her head, and

she shifted back another inch or so, the distance she put between us furrowing my brow and twisting my insides to hell.

"This is who I am, Pia." Voice raised, I slapped my cut, the fear of rejection rising to harden my voice. My heart. "I'm a callous, cold hearted fucking criminal, Pia. Have been since my teenage years when I ran with the Irish mob's goons."

She didn't open her mouth to reply, but I didn't give her time to.

"You know the cut I wear, know what I am. Don't act all surprised or disgusted by my giving the man just a taste of what he deserves. He's lucky I only broke his pretty face rather than slit his goddamn throat!"

My chest heaved, fire flooding through me.

Pia's face crumpled, and she reached out her hand for my leg.

I hopped up off the couch, hands fisted at my sides, my gut heaving with the need to empty my dinner battling the yearning for that caress she wanted to offer.

"You want something to touch?" I lashed out, yanking down my leather's zipper. "You said you'd be happy with this—well, this is all you're going to get from me, Pia. My dick."

She stood, quivering, tears replacing the pity that had shone in her eyes. "You're an asshole."

"Never pretended to be anything else, sweetheart," I said with a sneer, reaching into my leathers for my flaccid cock.

"You..." She spun away from me—needing more distance, and I couldn't fucking stand it. Couldn't have it.

I grasped her arm, spinning her back toward me, and she shied away with a gasp, her eyes wide, the fear in them knocking me on my goddamn ass.

"I won't hurt you," I heard myself say, all my focus on loosening my hold—and being unable to remove my fingers from her softness. Her warmth.

"I-I know." A shudder rippled down through her and a whimper escaped her trembling lips—and not the kind that came from arousal over my light hold remaining on her arm.

"Pia?"

Tears rolled down her cheeks, and it fucking hit me like a goddamn hammer to the head.

"Who hurt you?" I asked, my voice broken. Low as fuck—all anger ripping away at the need to protect her emotions, her mind.

"Foster father." Her whispered words tore my fucking heart to shreds.

"It's why you're such an advocate for those kids."

She managed to nod before breaking down, her hands over her face.

I dropped my hold on her arm and stood there like a goddamn idiot while she sobbed—same as Jenny that day I'd learned about the rape.

*We're both broken...*

But I was powerless to do a goddamn thing to help her. My jaw fucking ached, fingers clenched in fists at my sides as I waited, cursing myself a million times over in my head over being such a chicken shit.

Big tough biker ruled by fear.

She pulled in a few deep breaths, swiping at her tears, and finally stopped crying enough to wrap her arms around herself.

I stood like a goddamn buffoon, unmoving, unable to comfort her. Fucking broken asshole.

"I thought I'd found my forever home," she finally said, her gaze drifting toward the dark window beside us. "Sweet mother, kind-hearted father. Two younger kids I could maybe call step-siblings someday. It started out innocent enough. Pony tail tug. A pat on my shoulder when I came home with a good report card."

Pia sniffed, and I held my breath, wanting to

know it all—wanting to help carry her pain even if I couldn't reach to take it from her.

"We were a week into the adoption process when it happened the first time. He brushed too close against me for my liking. The second time, I asked him to not do it again—and that pissed him off."

A muscle ticked in my jaw as I fought off the spark of anger in my gut.

"It quickly escalated." She turned toward me, pain tugging on the corners of her eyes, but the resilient soul inside shown through. "It took my social worker three months to find me a new home when I'd begged for it. I never told her that he'd crept into my room twice and touched me, but then bruised me when I told him no. He always hurt me after that—but in places that would be hidden by clothes."

"Goddamnit, Pia," I managed through my clenched teeth.

"Once he realized I intended to fight off his advances, he never bothered with gentle touches. His fists, his digging fingertips, though, scarred me for years beyond the physical. That's the real reason I didn't let another man touch me until I was twenty-two. I couldn't stomach the idea of anyone's hands beneath my clothes."

I struggled to swallow against a range of emotions I couldn't even fucking name. "How'd you get over it?"

"I decided I wouldn't let that bastard ruin my life. It still took me a long time to get to second base with Phil, but he was patient. Helped me through without even knowing all the details of those months other than my vague explanation of having issues."

My goddamn gut clenched again. "You loved him."

A soft smile lightened her face and eased my insides the slightest bit. "My feelings for him don't compare to what I feel for you, Ryker."

## 20

# PIA

Ryker stared at me as though unsure of anything—his next breath, let alone words to use in reply to what I'd told him.

I knew he thought he'd scared me, that I feared his fists when he'd grabbed me, but that couldn't have been further from the truth. My instinctive reaction was to cringe, but only because of the sudden contact of skin—from *his* initiation, something I certainly hadn't expected.

His grip didn't scare me and neither did his lack of response.

Ryker had been nothing but kind to me, fiercely protective over his sister—and to a young woman he didn't even know.

No, I knew my cold hearted bastard would never abuse me. But did *he*?

"Do you fear becoming like him?" I asked as he continued to stare at me.

"I'm nothing like him," Ryker swore, his scowl returning.

"You're right. So, why fear touch?" I lifted my shirt off over my head and it dropped to the floor in a quiet swish before the plan that sparked in my head even took full clarity.

Ryker's focus flitted down to my chest, to the flush rising upward over my breasts.

I unhooked my bra and let it fall, my nipples pebbling as his gaze ate them up. Dampness grew between my thighs, and I pushed off my jeans, my hands starting to shake as butterflies took flight inside me.

His focus slipped to my fingers as I hooked them beneath the sides of my panties. He held his breath, his own fingers flexing at his sides.

I bent to push my panties to the floor and stood once more, completely bare before him. Vulnerable in the worst way—and loving every damn second of it.

"*You* touch *me*, Ryker," I whispered. "Put your hands on me—prove to yourself, your unconscious, that you're a gentle man."

He didn't meet my gaze as his throat worked to swallow. Muffled thumps of my heart beat in my ears over the tense silence between us.

Realizing he needed more help, I lifted my left breast. "Touch me, Ryker."

"Damnit, Pia," he whispered, his voice ragged. One stuttered step brought him close enough...

His hand shook as he raised it, and I bit back my gasp as his fingertip danced over my aching nipple.

"I need you," I whispered as he repeated the motion, sending a rush of wetness to coat my thighs. "You make me insane with desire. I'm so wet..."

He stepped back, his hands once more fisting, his stare between my thighs. "Bedroom," he rasped out, erasing the spring of disappointment his withdrawing had brought to life in my chest.

I turned and made for my bedroom, glancing over my shoulder to make sure he followed.

His gaze was glued to my ass as he slipped off his cut and ripped his shirt off overhead.

Broad shoulders ... muscled and thick ...

I bumped into my door jam and quickly turned back around, biting the inside of my lip to keep from giggling.

"How do you want me?" I asked, turning as I reached the foot of my bed.

"On your back."

He pushed down his leathers, not even bothering with ridding himself of his boots and the pants below his knees before following me up onto the bed.

## RYKER

My heart beat erratically as fuck as she laid back and spread her thighs, hands on the headboard.

"I won't touch you," she promised, so much emotion in her eyes, I had to give in to what we both craved. Fucking needed it even if my gut clenched in rebellion. I'd managed to touch her tit without vomiting—maybe I *could* do more.

I started with my breath held while kneeling between her thighs, one fingertip trailing up the inside of her calf. Satiny soft. Smooth and warm. Goosebumps broke over her skin, and her legs spread open farther, going lax on a sigh as I touched the inside of her knee.

*I can do this.*

Jaw clenched, I trailed toward the cream dripping from her slightly gaping pussy lips hiding what my dick throbbed for.

Pia was panting by the time I reached the apex of her thighs—the blonde hair, the protruding clit, something I'd never touched on a woman, but knew all about. Swollen labia, slick with need, and that droplet of arousal stretching toward the mattress.

I caught it with my finger and slid it back up through her slick, petal-soft slit, her whimper and the rise of her hips toward my touch too fucking much.

I planked and shoved in with one forward movement, stilling as she stared up at me, wide eyed, her pussy clamping down on my rigid shaft, sucking me deeper—fucking deeper than I thought possible.

Skin on skin.

Forgot the fucking condom in my lust to take her. Should have freaked out by the closeness, the lack of anything between us, but absolute heaven slammed into my brain.

"Touch me," she whispered again, and I pulled out, bent my head, and clamped my lips over her nipple.

"Oh!" She arched up in offering, and I slid back home, her wet heat enough to make my eyes roll back into my head.

*Fucking hell. Lug nuts and wrenches...*

*Don't fucking blow.*

I dragged out and flexed my ass, burying myself to the hilt.

*Ratchet sets and carburetors.*

I twirled my tongue around the hard nub between my lips, gently bit.

She shuddered beneath me, gyrating, definitely fighting the desire to wrap her body around mine.

Knowing my time ran short, I sat back abruptly, watching my dick disappear into her creamy pussy as I nudged forward while on my knees.

"Fucking beautiful," I stated with a groan. I wanted more. Needed to see more.

Gone to all thoughts but her, knowing her, seeing her, I grasped her thighs, spreading them wide, her skin so fucking addictive beneath my calloused palms. Pulling out to the tip hurt, but the lush feel of her body swallowing me back in...

"Not gonna fucking last, little lamb," I managed through clenched teeth.

"Help me, Ryker." She tossed her head to the

side, eyes clenched shut, her arms shaking from holding onto the headboard. "Please touch me —help me."

I pulled out halfway and slid a thumb up the back of my dick, crossing over to her skin where we joined, straight to her swollen clit.

"Tell me how to touch you," I rasped out, rubbing in circles, unable to even think about engine parts or fuck into her for fear of blowing my load too early.

"Just like that." She gasped and jerked at I pressed harder, her lower lip between her teeth.

I continued the action, enthralled by the concentration on her face, the noises coming from her shuddering chest. Dipping my fingers down once more, I gathered more wetness, leaning forward to plank on one arm while rubbing her hard nub.

"Need..." She licked her lips, her head thrashing. "Please."

I pushed in, teeth clenched as tingles started in my lower back.

Fucking doomed.

"Come around me, little lamb. Soak my cock, Pia ... fuck, I need to feel you come all over my dick."

"Ahh..." Her chest rose as she arched, mouth opened.

"Look at me."

Her eyelids lifted—and she climaxed with enough force around me, I saw fucking stars. I lost control. Head dipped, I watched my dick fuck into her with frantic thrusts, smashing her headboard against the wall—chasing the goddamn tingles shooting toward my balls.

I convulsed at the first spurt. Cursed myself for not pulling out. Thrust and unloaded more spunk, whispering her name as she cried out a second time, another rush of wetness, another spasm of her pussy sucking me deeper.

"Fuck!" I gasped for breath with the last twitch of my dick, head drooping between my shoulders, forehead on her chest, my heart pounding in my ears, her hot breath caressing my scalp. "Holy *fucking* hell."

"Okay?" she whispered, still breathless and keeping her hands to herself.

I realized she'd even managed to keep her heels on the bed.

"Yeah." I breathed out a heavy exhale. "Better than okay." I nibbled on her breast before pushing up—and trying to shove my semi deeper into her soaked pussy. "Fucking perfect."

I pulled out in a rush of cum, my brow furrowing. "Sorry about taking you bare."

"It's okay. I'm on the pill."

"I didn't mean to."

"It's okay, Ryker."

I nodded and rolled off the bed, hanging onto my pants to keep them from dropping to my ankles and tripping me as I made my way to the bathroom.

---

I laid on my side, watching Pia sleep. Lips parted, pink still flushing her cheeks. Seemingly innocent as a child ... how could a man steal from such kindness? Hurt such a sweet spirit?

A man like my father.

The muscle in my jaw ticked, but I forced myself to remain calm.

Pia had known abuse at the hands of the man who was supposed to help see her through to her adult years, same as I had but, unlike me, she'd chosen the high road. A life dedicated to helping the innocent ones like herself who didn't have a family to call their own.

I hadn't known respect for too many people in my life, but Pia topped them all. A warrior. A nurturing mother-type to those who needed one. An angel in human form with a heart of absolute fucking gold. She would make an unbelievable mother. That truth sent an ache through my chest.

A strand of her hair lay over her cheek, and I gently tucked it back, my fingertip brushing the top of her ear.

She didn't stir—and my gut didn't twist.

I'd been able to touch her. Fuck her face to face, three times, watch her eyes as she came around me. The possibilities ahead...

My chest tightened.

Possibilities, yes, but allowing such vulnerability could leave me in a worse place than where we'd started. It could fucking end me.

Pia was too good for me, and she would eventually realize that and take her affection away. The though made me want to vomit, but I couldn't pull myself from her bed to leave. I'd had no intentions of staying the night, but her whispered plea for me to stay had decided the rest of my evening. I considered the heart I thought I'd lost years earlier, the emotions and desires I had for more, letting me know it still beat hopefully inside my soul.

I feared rejection, but I feared losing her almost

as much. I hadn't had my fill of Pia Hill—I wanted more.

*I'm going to enjoy you just a little bit longer,* I whispered in my head while finally closing my eyes. *But I hope you don't hate me for keeping my heart locked away.*

## 22

## PIA

I woke before my alarm clock and glanced over to find Ryker on his back, breathing heavy. Stubble covered his head, and I settled on my side to study the man who had turned my entire world upside down and inside out.

He didn't believe he was a good man, and from the outside looking in, most of society would agree with his findings. But he'd allowed me inside. Allowed me a peek into his thought processes, his emotions that he didn't seem too fond of.

We'd made progress the night before, leaps and bounds beyond what I'd even hoped for, and he officially knew more about me than my closest friends. I'd flipped, unloaded all my dirty laundry—and he still stuck around when I'd feared he would leave. He'd let his walls down, even.

His touch, the little it was, had thrilled me, turned me on more than any man's had. I'd felt like a blushing virgin bride, experiencing arousal and lust for the first time.

Warmth between my thighs shifted my lower half on the mattress, and Ryker's breathing paused for a second.

I held still—but it was too late.

He turned his head, sleepy lids peeling upward, and the softness in his hazel eyes, the complete lack of shielding, made me want him all the more. The desire to roll on top of him, kiss us both breathless, and take him into my body shot adrenaline through me like sparks from a fire—crackling and ready to explode.

"Morning," I whispered instead, unable to keep from smiling as my insides jittered. I could wake up to him every morning without complaint...

"Morning," he grumbled, his rumbly voice pebbling my nipples. "Coffee."

I laughed outright and climbed out of bed, knowing from our time in Ogunquit there wouldn't be cuddles and morning sex. Coffee, the love of his life, it seemed, it would be. At least I had a French press and good grinds rather than single packet brewer bags like the hotel.

———

Ryker stayed the next night—business to take care of in Southie with his mom's condo and final legal details putting the place up for sale since Jenny had decided to stay in Vegas for the time being. I didn't ask, simply made him dinner when I got home and lost myself in his eyes when we'd ended up in bed, me beneath him, his fingertip touches more sure and with less hesitancy.

Still no kissing, but the hope I had bubbling inside me could float a fishing boat.

He invited me to spend the weekend at his place in Topsfield—spend the weekend at the club. Meet his brothers. Their old ladies.

His real family, he'd called them.

Giddiness lit me up from the inside, and not hugging his back as we sped up the highway on Friday night proved near impossible. Without saddle bags like Warden's bike, I ended up using my backpack, every nook and cranny stuffed full.

I allowed myself a few thigh brushes against his, and even brushed my elbow against his while we washed up the dinner dishes at his home late that evening.

And what a home, definitely more than a single man needed. I wondered if he'd bought it subconsciously thinking about his future, wanting a wife and children, but I didn't want to pry and put him on edge.

I'd never seen him so relaxed, and I wished for more of the same—for that would ensure even more progress between us.

That ease dissipated Saturday afternoon as we readied to head to the Viper's club. Tension ate at his shoulders, and his eyes glinted with wariness—concern for something. He brushed aside my question if he was alright, so I climbed onto the back of his bike once more, my own nerves rising.

He'd told me a handful of names, even mentioning Warden and his woman along with Stone and his new girl—and couldn't hide the envy in his voice. I didn't doubt at that point, he *did* wish for more. That he did yearn to live life like a normal man.

My desire, my determination to help him, tripled.

Regardless of what I would find at the Viper's den, I would stand by him—even if he wasn't yet my man.

## 23

## RYKER

Pia sat primly in the chair beside me at the table the officers lounged around. At least the music had lowered enough conversation wasn't difficult. Not that Warden or Stone would have noticed or cared. Both sat, legs sprawled, their women on their laps, lost in their own fucking worlds.

I had a beer in front of me rather than the whiskey my head and throat craved.

Pia brushed the back of her hand against mine where they both set atop the table, and I managed to not jerk away like an asshole. My shift in my chair betrayed my unease, though, and she mouthed a, "Sorry" to me.

I dipped my head to let her know no big deal—and Vigil caught my eye, his eyebrow raising.

A scowl dented my brow, and I slugged down a few swallows of my ice cold beer.

So fucking weak. Why couldn't I give in? Why couldn't I pluck Pia off her chair and settle her in my lap where I wanted her?

"Let's dance!" Shaun, Warden's woman, hopped off his lap, and I noted the catchy tune spilling out of the speakers as some new girly song she and Giada had been bellowing the last time I'd been back at the club.

"Come on!" Shaun grasped Pia's hand and pulled her up, and my brow smoothed as Pia cast me a quick, silly smile.

"Have fun," I grunted before drinking down the rest of my beer. My gaze locked on her ass as Shaun and Giada headed a few feet away to the open area they usually danced in.

"She's a good woman," Vigil noted.

"Don't I fucking know it." I glanced around the table quickly, calculating the refills we needed. "Bucky!" I held up five fingers to the pledge manning the bar, and he nodded.

"Too fucking good," I resumed the conversation, sitting back in my chair, hands on my thighs, my focus back on the woman I obsessed over.

"You let her touch your dick yet?" Devil asked,

and I flicked him the bird. "She touched your hand, and you didn't even flinch."

"Pretty fucking amazing, if you ask me," Warden tossed out. "Nice to see, Ryker."

I nodded, only half listening.

"You gonna put a ring on it?" Devil asked, and I glanced his way, scowling.

He sat back, hands raising. "Can't blame a brother for asking considering your past of making the whores keep their hands behind their back to suck you off."

He spoke truth, but that didn't make it any easier to hear.

"You fuck her face to face?"

I glared at Vigil—he alone knew I'd never had a woman that way in my forty-three years.

Our stare down lasted all of three seconds before he chuckled. "Well, goddamn." He grinned. "I'd slap your back to congratulate you, but I like my nose where it is."

I grunted something about his ugly mug that earned chuckles from around the table.

"You ought to claim her before she realizes what a cold hearted prick you are."

I stared over the table at Stone and his challengingly raised eyebrow, but kept my mouth shut. I'd watched him stab Arturo twice before slicing his throat—and he called me a cold hearted prick. Fucker hadn't shown an ounce of hesitation—and not a single one of remorse since.

"Well, I, for one, hope she sticks around long enough to crumble your walls." Warden grabbed the beer Bucky held out to him, and lifted it, watching and waiting as the prospect handed the other four bottles over. "To Ryker, the sick son-of-a-bitch whose callous ass just might allow the soft touch of a good woman."

"I'll drink to that!" Devil hooted, and Vigil dipped his head in agreement, less jovial while studying my face.

We clinked our bottles together over the center of the table—how couldn't I drink to what my heart longed for—and we guzzled down our drinks.

"She fits right in," Vigil observed, setting his bottle back on the table, and my focus turned toward the girls.

"She's also hot as fuck for you," Devil said. "Watches you like a hawk."

I wanted to argue it was her motherly-type instincts, but saying that out loud would probably sound weird as fuck.

"Fucking gone on you, if you ask me," Stone said.

"Not asking you." I swigged the colder brew, putting an end to the conversation.

"You ever call Klingon about watching over Jenny?" Stone asked a few seconds later.

"Yeah. He knows where she is and is watching out for her." He, like me, wasn't so sure she needed a full-time body guard, and I didn't want to worry Jenny with things she had no business knowing. We'd agreed to keep things quiet, but his chapter would have her back undercover, unless something blew up in our faces.

"Jenny must love Pia—putting up with your grumpy ass," Devil said with a chuckle, starting up the goddamn ribbing again.

I ignored their shit for as long as possible, watching Pia dance, watching her watch me, but within fifteen minutes, I'd had enough—especially once the women returned and the face sucking started up.

I roared my bike's engine to life, and Pia and I took off out of the compound, heading north, back home.

We weren't in the kitchen ten seconds before she stepped in front of me, blocking me from escaping. Luminous eyes peering up at me, face flushed from dancing and riding, she all but begged to be bent over the island. Fucked to within an inch of her life.

She lifted her hand, and I held my breath, allowing her to touch my beard. "You hoped for a fuller future when you bought this place, didn't you?"

I grunted—she could take it however the hell she wanted.

"I saw your jealousy over Warden and Stone's ease with their women. You long for that, too, don't you?"

"I dreamed of having a few rug rats of my own one day," I let loose with the truth, because why the fuck not? Telling her my desires wasn't the same as putting my heart on a fucking platter for her to stab to death.

"Stupid," I muttered when she didn't respond.

"No." She dropped her hand but didn't take her focus off my mouth. "It's not stupid in the least. If you don't have hopes and dreams, what's the point of living? That would be an empty existence, I think. Boring and lonely."

I didn't move an inch, just stood there like a goddamn buffoon while she stared at my lips, her own desire all too easy to read. Dilating pupils, parting lips, breath coming faster as the pulse in her neck heightened.

"What do you hope for, Pia?" I heard myself ask, needing to burrow into her head like I wanted to do to her body with every inch of my skin against hers.

"That you'll kiss me some day." She lifted her focus to my eyes, peering deep inside my goddamn soul—probably seeing the chest I'd locked my heart up inside. "Think you could?" she whispered.

I realized I'd reached out—that my palm rested on her curvy hip, without thought, without intent. My sub-conscious and body sure as fuck wanted her.

"I won't kiss you back, Ryker—promise. But I need to feel your lips on mine."

Fucking temptation to give the fuck in...

My dick jerked to attention at the thought of having her on my lap, our mouths fused as she rode my cock...

*Fuck it.* If I flipped out from a simple kiss and scared her off, she'd be gone before weaseling my heart out of its cage.

I leaned down and gave Pia what she wanted.

## 24

## PIA

I held my breath, beyond surprised he moved in on me, and at the slight brush of his lips across mine, I lost myself to him, my ovaries singing hallelujah and then some. Holding still hadn't ever been so hard, and I trembled, my heart *pounding* as he slid the soft cushion of his mouth over mine once more.

Ryker pulled back, blinking, his attention glued to my moistened lips. My heart soared, and I couldn't keep my smile contained.

"Again," I told him.

He swallowed, but leaned down.

My cell rang in my back pocket—Stacey's ringtone I'd assigned her to know if Dasia ever happened to call.

I wanted Ryker's lips on me, but Dasia…

"I'm sorry." I turned away and dug my cell out of my back pocket. I heard her sobs before I even got the phone to my ear. "Dasia?" I stepped back fully, my heart in my throat.

"He raped me!"

A shudder rippled over me, and I sagged against the island, clutching it with my free hand. "Ted Griffey?"

"Yes!" She sobbed, and I could make out Stacey murmuring in the background.

*No. Please God.* I choked on my own sob, fighting for calm, fighting to remain upright and not spew the contents of my stomach all over Ryker's kitchen.

"He said he couldn't help himself," she managed to say between her hysterics. "Said his demons wouldn't leave him alone."

"Are you at Stacey's?" I asked, my stomach still churning.

"Yes."

"You have to go to the hospital, Dasia. Report this."

"No—I can't."

"You have to!"

"I'm taking off the second I hang up," she said, her voice calming the slightest as my insides heaved.

"Please don't come looking for me—I need you to leave me go this time, Miss Pia. Please."

"Dasia, please, don't do this."

She didn't reply, and I forced my eyelids open to glance at my cell.

She'd hung up.

My stomach heaved again, and I dropped my phone, sprinting toward the bathroom. The first spew from my lips splattered on the tile floor alongside the toilet. The rest of my stomach contents landed where I'd intended, and tears poured from my eyes.

I dry heaved, sobbing, the sense of failure, of absolute powerlessness flooding through me.

Warmth lay on my lower back—Ryker's hand—but I found no joy in the fact he'd found the strength to comfort me.

I sank to the clean side of the toilet and curled into a ball.

"What happened?" Ryker asked with such tenderness, more tears poured down my face to drip to the floor.

"He raped her," I choked out, surprised he hadn't heard her over the phone.

Curses spewed from his lips, and in that moment of time, I didn't care if he left me, sped to Boston and sliced the fucker's throat. Ted Griffey deserved to die a horrible death—but he deserved to have his dick sliced off and shoved up his ass before breathing his last.

---

We did speed southward in his truck that night, but a call through to Stacey let me know Dasia had gone—and she hadn't told her friend where she was headed.

"For my own sake," Stacey said, her voice as forlorn as the heaviness in my chest.

"Do your parents know?" I asked, staring unseeing at the dark landscape outside the passenger window.

"No—they were out to dinner with friends when Dasia came over."

"What happened?" I forced myself to ask.

"I-I didn't ask. She just showed up with a bruised cheek, sneakers untied, in shorts and a tank top."

I closed my eyes and tipped my head back. "She didn't give you any hint about where she was going to go?"

"None."

A heavy sigh emptied my lungs, and sucking air

back in hurt. "Did you give her other clothes to wear?"

"A backpack full."

"Money?"

"I stole a few hundred from my dad's stash in his desk he doesn't think I know about."

"And what will you tell him when he finds it missing?"

"I'll say I took it for myself."

"If you hear from her at all or remember anything she said that might give her plans away, please call me."

"I will, Miss Pia. Promise."

"You're a good friend, Stacey."

"Not good enough to make her stay." Her voice broke, and feeling the same, I couldn't offer comfort.

I hung up and pressed the heels of my palms to my eyes, fighting off more tears and nausea.

"Nothing," I muttered, and Ryker remained silent as he'd been almost since Dasia had called.

"I failed her." Tears choked off my voice—and two slid simultaneously down my cheeks as Ryker reached over to grasp my hand.

"We'll find her," he rasped out, and I clung to the single bubble of hope his touch, his words, instilled inside me.

We drove around downtown, scoping the streets while waiting for Devil, the sneaky man, to hack into all sorts of places he had no business going.

She hadn't hopped a bus heading out of town. No airplane ticket showed up under her name.

While she did have her license, I doubted she would steal a car to make her escape.

Or would she?

We stopped by Dunks and I managed to talk the manager into giving me Jesse's number. He hadn't heard from her, but promised to make some calls and put the word out.

Twice, Ryker stopped at bars and disappeared inside for a few minutes. I knew he had contacts from his younger days in Southie, and thankfulness for him almost overrode my sense of failure.

At two in the morning, I told him to take me home. We fell asleep on either side of the bed, our hands clasped in between us.

I woke from the same dream I'd had earlier that week, and my churning stomach had me on my knees in front of my own toilet. I managed to swallow down the rising nausea, but didn't attempt to leave the bathroom for a full ten minutes.

Ryker met me with a cup of coffee—and my alarm went off.

Monday morning. Work at the stifling office.

I wanted to sob, but stuck my shoulders back and forced myself to face the world—and the shit that would hit the fan if I decided to open the can of worms. Useless, really. With Dasia gone and Ted Griffey being who he was, what could I possibly hope to accomplish?

Nothing.

Ryker told me he would do all he could, and that he would call me later.

I needed a kiss goodbye, a quick hug and assurance everything would be okay. I got neither, and I left for work. Alone in my old Chevy. Heartbroken and defeated.

## 25

# RYKER

olding onto my rage for twelve hours was a record for me. I'd cursed when Pia had told me what happened, but I didn't punch a wall. Didn't make a single call to Vigil when I so badly wanted to.

The second she drove off for work, though, I hit speed dial, watching through her living room window as she turned a corner and disappeared from sight.

I'd made myself a plan while Pia had slept through the night, but with the severity of my plan, I knew I needed to talk to Vigil first.

Once I filled him in on the phone call from Dasia, I didn't hold back telling him I planned on ripping Griffey's ball sack from his body with my bare hands. She wasn't my kid, and I didn't know Dasia personally, but that fucker had hurt Pia by his actions. I wouldn't stand for it. Sure as fuck wouldn't sit for it either.

"Bring him here." Vigil's cold tone brooked no argument.

Cold, completely cut off from all emotion, I agreed—and rang Devil to cover my ass.

I glanced at the time on my cell once I hung up, and high tailed it back to Pia's bedroom to grab the rest of my clothes.

Ted Griffey always headed into work at nine, sharp—and I knew his assigned parking spot and the fucking genius computer whiz to shut every goddamn security down with the press of a key.

Snagging him in broad daylight would be easy as fuck.

His end? Definitely wouldn't be easy.

———

I ripped off the hood I'd tied over his head and slapped his face, ready for him to wake from the bash against the head that still tingled my hand.

"Let me." Vigil stepped past me and dumped ice

water over the fucker's head, soaking his blond locks.

He twitched. Groaned.

"Wake the fuck up," I barked, kicking his shin as hard as I could.

Griffey jerked upward in the chair, his eyes blinking open. "Ung..." he groaned around the gag stuffed in his mouth and held in place by duct tape.

I kicked him again, and he cursed, his wince only the first taste of satisfaction I planned on bleeding from his body. I scowled as his head drooped once more.

Vigil rounded the chair we'd tied him to, arms crossed, his focus on my face. He nodded, giving me the green light.

I'd brought Griffey back to the Viper's compound, bound and gagged, passed the fuck out, in the second seat of my extended cab where I usually kept tools and shit. I was lucky he'd stayed out so long even though I'd had every intention of pulling over to bash his head again if he woke.

I'd hit him hard enough the second he climbed from his car in the parking garage, that I likely jostled his brain. Too hard, really, but my rage had gotten in the way. I was lucky he lived.

He wouldn't much longer, though.

The low building at the back of the compound housed the cleaners things along with an incinerator for the stuff that couldn't be wiped from existence when shit went down and we had stuff that needed to disappear. There were even a few freezers in the back room where we'd had to stuff a body or three for a time before getting rid of evidence of our criminal ways.

The Vipers weren't named Vicious for shits and giggles. If a fucker messed with what belonged to us, or inadvertently hurt one of our own, they paid.

Period.

Vigilante justice, the doling out of punishment I fucking lived for. Outlaw bikers at their fucking best.

"Wakey wakey, cocksucker," I stabbed my knife through his hand tied to the wooden chair.

Griffey screamed, blinking the haze from his eyes quick as fuck.

"There." I grinned although the joy in me banked on psychotic as I yanked my blade from between bones. "Now we can chat."

He blinked up at me with a deep groan, and I ripped the duct tape from off his head with one jerk, taking along some hair and a sweet as fuck scream.

"How ya like them apples?" I asked, holding up the gag with his pretty locks plastered to it. "Bet those goddamn demons inside you aren't too helpful right now are they?"

Recognition lit in his gaze seconds before the stench of piss reached my nose. He fucking whimpered. "Please ... I didn't mean to hurt her. You have to believe me!"

"You sick fuck." I spit at his face, and he closed his eyes, crying like a pussy. "I told you not to touch her, but your weak-assed pussy self couldn't keep your dick in your pants."

"Please."

I'd heard countless similar pleadings, and not a one had ever cracked through the thick callouses lining my soul. "Please?" I snorted a laugh and twirled my knife in my hand. "You really think I'm going to take it easy on you, you sick fuck?"

"I'll give you money—whatever you want!"

I nodded at Vigil and leaned in close once he'd yanked the fucker's head back by the hair. The stench of Griffey's fear fed the animal inside me. "What I want," I whispered while digging the tip of my blade into his cheek and he shrieked, "is to bleed you little by little."

I dug into his other cheek. "Crush one bone at a

time. Peel the fucking skin off your body until the pain is what takes you to the depths of hell where you soul belongs."

His screams erupted louder—and didn't stop until three hours later.

## 26

## PIA

Dasia had disappeared once more without a trace, and my hands were tied. She'd become nothing but another number, a statistic in a system that failed time and again.

I told myself it wasn't my fault—but I also cursed myself for not taking her in without the state's knowledge. I should have hid her in my own home, consequences be damned. She'd ended up paying the price for my mistake, and I couldn't forgive myself.

I didn't hear from Ryker all that day, and he wasn't at my apartment when I got home, exhausted and still half-sick. He didn't answer his cell, so I left a message asking him to please call me, before passing out in my bed.

The next morning, disappointed to be waking alone, I turned on the TV while making my coffee, dreading hearing about a young woman's body being found in some alleyway—same as I'd done for months after Sophia's disappearance and those weeks Dasia had taken off the first time.

An hour later, I sat, hands clasped in my lap to keep them from shaking, my coffee churning in my stomach.

Ted Griffey had gone missing, and his tearful wife didn't say a damn word about the foster girl who had left them the day before.

I swallowed—and lost the fight with my nausea, sprinting to the bathroom.

Did Mrs. Griffey know what he'd done to Dasia? Did she think the two had fallen in love and run off together?

I knew what he'd done—but so did a self-proclaimed cold hearted criminal I knew all-too well.

After cleaning up, I tried his cell, my hands shaking.

He didn't answer.

Tuesday, Mr. Griffey's disappearance remained in the news, and Ryker still hadn't returned my call.

Rumors abounded about his having countless

affairs—two women came forward to tell their story. Even more rumors rose about his taking off for Europe with his latest lover.

Wednesday came, and I found myself hugging my toilet once more.

Thursday, the same.

Friday, I sat back on my heels after vomiting, swiping the back of my hand over my mouth, eyes clenched shut, silently cursing myself.

Stress had often got the best of me and roused nausea, but never so many days in a row.

I placed my hand on my belly and knew what caused my sickness even though it hadn't been nearly long enough for me to be sick already. The condom he'd used the first time we'd had sex must have had a hole, *and* my birth control must have failed.

An hour later, two little lines appeared on the stick that cost me too damn much, telling me what I didn't really need confirmed.

I carried Ryker's baby.

———

That night, I sat on my couch, hugging my pillow against my belly, staring out into the darkness, complete silence reigning over my apartment. I wanted to tell Ryker—needed to, but I couldn't. I hadn't tried him all day, but he hadn't called, either.

Was he done with me?

Had that bit of comfort he'd offered me on Sunday night been too much for him to handle?

He hadn't touched me at all Monday morning, even avoiding my fingers when I took the coffee cup he'd held out to me. He'd been closed off, but so had I, too overcome with anxiety over Dasia to consider what he might be feeling.

Jenny had been raped.

Surely Dasia's had hit him as would news of any other young woman's abuse would have.

I'd failed him, too. Failed to note his emotional reaction. Failed to make sure *he* was okay in the mess I found myself in.

I closed my eyes, my throat tight, wishing hope bubbles that I guessed wrong about Mr. Griffey's disappearance would spring to life.

A knock sounded, and I heaved a sigh, expecting my elderly neighbor needed a cup of sugar—something she inquired over at least one a month. I peered out the peep hole, and my breath stalled out.

Ryker.

He hunched in a bulky gray sweatshirt, his gaze

lowered, his head covered by a few days' worth of scruff.

I wanted to talk to him, yet I didn't...

I unlocked and pulled open the door.

He let out a heavy breath as he lifted his head and focused on my lips. "Pia."

Unsmiling, I stepped back and motioned him in.

"How are you?" he asked as I shut the door behind him.

"We need to talk." I moved around him to the living room and curled back up in my corner, pillow against my belly.

He sat slowly—warily, almost, without meeting my gaze.

"Ryker. Look at me."

He lifted his head, and I knew.

So much for those hope bubbles. My heart sank, but I still needed his words of confirmation. "It was you, wasn't it?"

"Yes."

My throat swelled quick as lightning, and I clasped a hand over my mouth to keep from sobbing with disappointment, with pissiness, with bitterness, and every other imaginable emotion a pregnant woman does.

"I never lied about what I was, Pia."

"You're a murderer!" I half-shrieked, beyond rational, regular hormonal thinking.

"The fucker deserved it," he bit out, his eyes hardening to steel. "Just like the man who stole my sister's innocence!"

Confession from his lips.

I stared, tears rolling down my face, every feeling I'd had for him, every emotional connection, straining tight against the reality I carried a killer's baby. My stomach didn't care for the truth, and I hopped up, hurrying for the bathroom, tears rolling once more.

"Pia!"

"Just leave!" I hollered, slamming the bathroom door and dropping to my knees as vomit spewed from my between my lips.

I gagged. Heaved. Whimpered and bit back sobs.

"Pia?" Ryker said through the door, but I clenched my eyes shut against the fear, the hurt inflected in his voice.

"Go," I whisper-groaned loud enough he would hear.

Minutes later, my straining ears made out the front door clicking shut, and I broke down once more in a hormonal pity-party I felt I deserved.

## 27

## RYKER

I stayed away out of uneasiness that crept over me for hours after finally slitting Griffey's throat. No guilt over ending the fucker's life, but fear over the fact I knew Pia wouldn't approve, wouldn't understand my need to end him. I didn't doubt she would figure it out.

From the first news alert of his disappearance, I worried. Acid ate at my stomach, and I didn't have the balls to return Pia's calls. For almost the entire week, I'd been tempted to drink whiskey like water, but thoughts of how my father's downward spiral started kept me from even starting.

I might be a murderer, but I refused to be a man without control.

By Friday night, I couldn't fucking deal any more.

I needed to hear her voice, needed to talk to her, see her, hell, I even felt the need to touch her—beyond with my dick.

So much for that goddamn control, but at least it had been for a woman rather than oblivion.

I'd shown up at her apartment looking for comfort. Needing the calm she brought—and she set me aside.

Didn't want me.

Fucking broke the heart I thought I'd kept locked up.

I made some calls before leaving Southie, though, hitting up a few of my old crew guys, hiring them to keep an eye on her, her goings, her doings. I also returned two days later during the night to put a tracker on her car so Devil could keep watch, too, if needed.

Through it all, I remained sober as fuck, coffee my best friend, my only companion while at home.

Two weeks. Two fucking long as fuck weeks, I stayed away like she'd told me to do, and my insides withered up to a husk, empty and dead.

She never went to the police, and no badged assholes showed up looking for the remains of Ted Griffey, which they wouldn't have found anyway. We'd incinerated the shit out of him, the clothes and boots both Vigil and I had worn along with the cleaners' clothes after chemical-spraying down the entire interrogation room tossed in after he'd burned to nothing but unrecognizable bits. The ashes, we had a brother take out in the ocean and sprinkle into the wind while racing down the coastline.

There was nothing left of Ted Griffey except the broken-hearted wife who was better off without him, and the young woman he'd raped. Wherever she was.

Devil couldn't find her, so I knew no one would unless she turned up on her own.

None of my contacts in Southie had seen or heard a thing.

Into the third week of fucking hell, one of my guys called me up, the one I had tailing her to and from work every day like the obsession, protective prick I couldn't help but be.

"What's up?" I asked, striding into the chop shop's office, leaving Sully to the blow torch I'd been using when my cell had vibrated in my back pocket.

"Nothing serious," my man said, "but you told me to call if she did anything out of the ordinary—she went to the doctor's office this morning instead of work."

"What doctor?"

He paused for a second. "Porter OBGYN the sign on the door says."

All women had a yearly check-up—but the memory of her vomiting at my house over the news of Dasia, then vomiting again when I'd shown up at her house… Pia hadn't ever mentioned a sensitive stomach and never once seemed upset to the point of nausea when dealing with the Dasia situation before she'd run away.

A fucking light bulb went off in my head, tightening my chest and making me dizzy.

I sat in my office chair. "Follow her afterward and text me where she goes," I managed to toss out before hanging up.

If what I concluded was true, she'd be hitting up a pharmacy for those horse pills Warden told me Shaun started on the week before.

Prenatal. Warden was going to be a father.

I should have feared becoming one myself, but I didn't. The fact I had a chance to prove to myself I was nothing like the bastard who raised me, a chance to redeem my bloodline, sparked something inside my head. The cracked heart lying inside that damn chest like looted pirate booty began to beat again.

A text dinged, and I glanced down, realizing I'd been staring at the office's gray wall for over an hour.

**Pharmacy.**

Sure I was right, I packed up my shit for the day and headed out, Sully's big wave following me out the door.

An hour later, knowing Pia had gone to work after the pharmacy and a quick stop at home, I jimmied my way into her apartment. The fruity scent of her flooded my nose, and I stood inside the door, noting the changes she'd made since I'd been there.

The couch had been angled more toward the windows which new drapes framed. A new rug lay beneath my feet, and different coffee mugs hung on the hanger thing she had sitting beside the French press.

Best damn coffee I'd ever tasted. Fuck, had I missed it.

I moved into her bedroom. New bedspread. Plumper pillows.

Had she been trying to erase the memory of me? The scent I might have left behind on her bedding? Or had she decided she needed a fresh start for her and our child?

An actual growl sounded in my chest.

My gaze landed on the bed stand. A book on what to expect when you're pregnant sat there, confirming my thoughts.

A well of protectiveness rose inside me like a goddamn swell, ready to knock down anything or anyone stopping me from reaching my fate's shore—Pia. She carried my kid. She was my woman.

And both of them were mine, whether she liked it or not.

No word from Dasia.

No word from Ryker.

Not that I expected any from either. The hurt I'd seen on Ryker's face as I'd spewed out in hysterics over his being a murderer let me know my words had done damage I hadn't truly intended. Over two weeks had passed, and every morning that I hugged the damn porcelain god, dry heaving my innards up, I wished for his presence.

The apartment felt so empty without him, my bed cold. My heart, even colder. I couldn't even sum up excitement over knowing I would have a child, that I would have the chance to lavish love on a little soul all my own. Give that baby everything I'd never had. Spoil it rotten with hugs, kisses, and love.

For the first time in my life, I had my own forever home—made real by the tiny heartbeat I'd heard.

It had been one hell of a long Monday from getting my first ultrasound and hearing the baby's heartbeat to going to work and finding I had three new clients needing homes. Add in stopping at the grocery store on the way home for a few things, and I wanted nothing more than to collapse and sleep straight through the night.

By the time I parked my car outside my apartment, darkness descended like a heavy blanket, and I cursed the time of year when the nights began to overshadow the afternoon.

It was going to be a long, lonely winter full of ice cream and pickles. I hadn't began the craving thing yet, but I expected it wouldn't be long before I packed on the pounds.

I trudged up the stoop, two bags of groceries in my hands. The door swung inward before I could put them down to fish my keys from my purse.

Ryker stood inside my apartment's doorway, face deadpan, eyes shuttered—wary.

"What are you doing in my house?" I squeaked out, and he took the bags from me without answering.

I followed him inside and shut the door behind

me before slipping off my light coat. Morning sickness still plagued me, but at least I wasn't puffed up like a fat cow, yet.

He set the groceries aside and turned to face me, waiting for me to hang my coat in the tiny closet and put my purse on the table where I usually left it.

"If you think you can just toss me out of your life, not giving me a say, you've got another think coming."

I stared at him, beyond exhausted. "I don't have the energy for this right now."

"Is it mine?"

He knew. Somehow, he'd found out—I shouldn't have been surprised.

"Yes," I whispered, wrapping my arms around myself.

"Will you keep it?"

"Yes."

His shoulders lowered a little, my answer alleviating stress I hadn't realized rode him. His eyes softened, and he held out his hand.

Hope bubbled up inside me, and I couldn't find it in myself to care about what he'd done. I pushed aside thoughts of his criminal actions and peered up at the man whose heart shone in his eyes. The heart I'd come to learn existed in his hardened shell. The softness and hatred of vulnerability he hid from the world.

My eyes stung—damn hormones.

"I don't hurt people that don't deserve it," he said, his voice low but steady. "Yes, I've used these hands to do bad things, but I want to learn how to use them for good. Show me, Pia. Give me a chance."

I swallowed against the tightness in my throat.

"I want to learn how to touch you—how to hold our child someday. I want to be able to give them the affection my father refused me when I begged for it."

A sob broke from me.

What could I do but nod? I loved him with every part of me, regardless of his past, and he offered me the chance to press my ear to his chest and drown in his heartbeat.

# RYKER

Tears rolled from her eyes, but she gave me the green light.

Teeth clenched, I moved in, focusing on my love for her—yes, fucking love—and the similar emotions I could see in her wet eyes. I clenched my eyelids shut and wrapped my arms around her, pulling her softness against my chest.

A heavy sigh escaped her as she melted against me, arms by her sides, but allowing me to hold her, her cheek against my chest. My sweet, discerning woman simply rested. Submitted. Her sniffles continued as I breathed in the sweetness of watermelon, continuing to focus all my thoughts on her—our baby—rather than the clenching in my gut.

I would beat the fucking fear one day. Rip it from

my goddamn head and burn it to a fucking crisp. It held no authority in my life. I refused to allow it to fuck up my chance at the future I'd only ever dreamed about.

"You're holding me," Pia whispered without moving her cheek from my chest, and I realized her tears had stopped.

"Yeah," I said, my voice all gruff and pansy-assed. I cleared my throat. "Feels pretty fucking amazing."

Pia tipped her head back, her focus lingering on my eyes for a few seconds—reading my goddamn soul, most likely—before dropping to my lips.

"Can I kiss you?" I asked, knowing where her mind went, that thought stirring my dick to life.

"Only if I can kiss you back." She returned her attention on my eyes, the challenge tossed out with a firm voice.

Fuck baby steps. I'd taken enough of the goddamn things—and they'd gotten my woman knocked up. I decided it was time to jump in and see how much I could take without flipping the fuck out.

I leaned down and pressed my mouth to the soft cushion of hers, a deep groan vibrating in my chest.

My little lamb kept her hands to herself, but nothing else. She kissed me back, flicked her tongue along the seam of my mouth, and I let her in, soaking up her whimpers, breathing in her exhales, drawing her so damn deep into my lungs she'd always be a part of me.

I'd been missing heaven for over forty years. Even my stomach relaxed while I drowned in my very first ever *real* kiss. No wonder Warden and Stone couldn't keep from sucking their woman's faces off.

*Goddamn.*

Pia rubbed against my aching dick, drawing another groan from me. She pulled back, putting a finger to my lips when I chased after her mouth like the greedy bastard I'd suddenly become.

"I need you inside me, Ryker."

She tugged my arm from the band around her back and I let go—not too willingly. A giggle escaped her as she laced her fingers through mine and tugged me back down the hallway.

We stood in silence, drinking the sight of each other up while stripping down to bare skin. A flush covered Pia's chest, her face, her nipples tight and begging for my teeth. She finished first thanks to my damn boots, and I stared as she sat on the bed, legs parted enough I could see a hint of wetness on her pussy lips.

"Whatever you want," she whispered, "however

you need me to be. I want this, Ryker. I don't give a shit what you are, who your brothers are. I want *you.* Every awful, beautiful part."

*Fuck, I'm a goner.*

Once rid of my boots and jeans, I kissed my way up her legs rather than feather my fingertips over her satiny skin. The scent of the wetness dampening the curls atop her pussy drove me fucking insane, and for the first time in my life, I took a long, slow as hell lick of the most addictive silkiness on the goddamn planet.

Tangy, salty, and yet sweet, Pia's arousal flooded my senses. Taste buds. The musky scent of her filling my nose and turning me light-headed as fuck as all the blood rushed to my straining dick.

I kissed up over her pubic bone and back down, nudging my nose through the curls and over her clit.

"Goddamn, woman," I muttered, nosing up her soft belly, her legs widening for my hips as I slid higher.

Tits for fucking days... I lifted them together and buried my face between them, breathing in her skin as she shifted and panted beneath me. Not one fucking ounce of acid burned in my gut.

"Ryker..."

I lifted my head from rubbing my beard and

cheeks against her tits to find her grasping the head-board, her face a gorgeous shade of pink, her lips parted and eyes luminous in the overhead lights.

Shifting higher, I planked—and slid fucking home. To the goddamn hilt, in one easy glide.

"Fuck." I hissed through clenched teeth as her pussy contracted as though trying to pull me deeper. I pulled out. Slid back in—but I hadn't yet reached my limit on skin. I wanted more.

"Put your legs around me, Pia."

She obeyed without hesitation, but brushed my hips with the insides of her thighs gently, giving me time to adjust.

"Higher," I said through clenched teeth while flexing my ass and burying deep again.

Skin. So much goddamn skin. Softness. Satiny fucking *heaven*.

God, the things I'd been missing out on all because of fucking PTSD and fear.

Pia locked her heels behind my ass and pulled me back in after I'd dragged out, trying to memorize the slick grasp of her pussy.

"Keep your hands there," I told her while leaning down, my words whispered over her lips.

"I will."

I pressed my lips to hers, and got so damn caught

up in the swell of emotion, need, that I forgot my name. Forgot everything but her, the sweetness of watermelon, the slickness of her tight sheath, the taste of her on my lips.

*Mine. My woman. My life—my fucking future.*

My hips jolted with frantic thrusts, and the second before I exploded, she gasped against my mouth, her pussy clamping down on me like a vise. My balls released, spurting deep inside her, coating her—claiming her.

30

## PIA

I thought I'd been exhausted when I'd gotten home, but Ryker had wrecked me in the best way possible. I passed out seconds after he used a warm, wet towel to clean between my legs. Dreamless. Dark. Peaceful.

Waking came easy as I felt refreshed for the first time in weeks.

Ryker lay on his side facing me, his eyes already open and alert as though he'd been watching me for some time. One of his hands clasped over mine in the space between us.

Full to bursting had a whole new meaning for me, and I smiled, wanting nothing more than to stay in bed with him for the rest of our lives, taking new steps, progressing to the point there would be no limits, no restrictions between us.

I realized my hands still ached from clenching the head board with every bit of strength and stubbornness I had the night before.

"I'm proud of you," I whispered, knowing we'd get beyond my hands staying to myself someday.

"I'm a bad man."

"You're also protective—passionately so, and I love that about you. I mean, there's a lot I love about you—I'm falling *in* love with you," I blurted and snapped my jaw shut.

Ryker studied me without a flicker of emotion on his face, his entire body still.

"I know it's quick," I couldn't help but rush to fill the silence, "but you're cautious, courageous, observant, and whether you admit to it or not, you've got a heart of gold—"

He captured my mouth, shutting me up, spinning my brain, and waking up the hormonal beast inside me who couldn't seem to get enough of him.

"I'm fucking dead gone on you, woman," he grumbled, pulling back enough to peer into my eyes, his fingers tightening their hold on mine even though we didn't touch in any other way. "You're mine now. No changing your fucking mind, leaving me, and ripping my goddamn heart out of my chest, got it?"

"You're going to have to clean up your mouth when the baby arrives."

Ryker snorted. "Don't fucking count on it."

"I'm serious."

"And you can kiss my ass."

Biting back a smirk, I touched his beard lightly with my free hand. He didn't pull away—he didn't reach for me, either. But, I had patience, and his touch, his affection I'd gotten a taste of, promised to be worth the wait.

"So, now what?" I asked, searching his face.

"You're moving in with me."

"Just like that?"

"Yep."

I considered what to say even though I knew my mind had been made up the first minute I'd grasped his arm outside Dunks. "What about my work?"

"You'll have your own kid to nurture now."

"And if I want to work outside the home to help those who *aren't* mine?"

"Then do it. Just closer than Boston. Near our home."

"Home." I smiled too wide for pre-dawn hours. "I think I'd like that."

"Good." He grunted and rolled off the bed, my fingers cooling without his warmth.

"Where are you going?"

"Coffee."

I laughed lightly. I should have known.

## 31

## RYKER

A FEW WEEKS LATER

"How's it going, daddy-o?"

I flicked Devil off, watching Pia and Shaun across the club pouring over baby magazines. We'd painted the second bedroom a sage green and she'd hung white, light-blocking blinds, frilly lace-type material along the top to make it pretty.

Pretty. Whatever she wanted, I hopped aboard, even if the little shit was a boy. She'd glared at me over the nickname, so I made sure to keep that one inside my head whenever referring to the little avocado-sized McGrath growing in her belly.

My house no longer felt like a cold shell. Pia had brought warmth, her books, her knickknacks scattered all over the place. I didn't mind one bit.

I fucking *lived* for the first time in over forty years,

"Got names picked out yet?"

I finally glanced over at Devil. He sat brooding over a beer while I drank a tonic. I'd given up alcohol for good. No point in drinking at all and getting wasted even on beer when I had responsibilities more important than my own selfish desires.

"We're going to find out what it is first," I answered, wondering over the usually happy-go-lucky's lack of fascial expression.

He nodded and swigged, his focus on the two women as well. "You know, seeing that gives me hope."

"What's that?"

"That I can find someone who fits me as well as Pia does you."

"I think there's someone out there for everyone," I told him a bit gruff, trying to hide my new pansy-assed side. "Even your twisted, fucked-up head."

"I'm not fucked up," he muttered and sipped again.

"Don't argue that twisted part though, do you?"

He tipped his head to the side and shrugged. "Nothing wrong with a little kink to exorcise the demons."

"Never said there was. Aren't there clubs and shit you could go to? Those secret places down in Boston that'll take thousands from your pockets so you can tie women up for your sick pleasure?"

"It's not just for my pleasure, you callous prick." He scowled. "It's all about giving a submissive what she needs."

"Call it what you will." I lifted my tonic. "Just saying that shit isn't for everyone, but there are those out there willing to pay for it if you really want to go find them."

My cell vibrated, and I pulled it from my back pocket. The guard at the front gate—one of the prospects hoping to get his patch within the month.

"What's up?" I spoke into my cell while glancing toward the window even though I wouldn't see the gate from the angle.

"There's a woman out here asking for your old lady."

I frowned, glancing over at Pia. "She give you a name?" I asked, remembering all-too well the night Ben Thode and his daughter Shaun had shown up asking for Warden.

"Won't give me her name, but she's beat up pretty bad. Looks like she's walked a long fucking way in the cold, too. You better get out here."

"Shit." I hung up and stood, motioning toward the door with my head when Devil glanced up at me.

"What's up?" he asked, setting his beer aside and hopping to his feet.

"Someone at the gate, and you're the only other officer here right now, so you'd better come along."

"Who?" he asked, following on my heels across the club.

I shoved open the front door and caught Pia's eye before stepping outside. Curiosity lit her gaze, but I didn't show any emotion. Didn't want to set her nerves on end.

"Not sure," I muttered to Devil before stepping outside.

A few strides across the parking lot took me close enough to the gate I recognized the young redhead.

"Roll it open!" I barked at the prospect, my focus glued to Dasia.

Battered and bruised, a little hunched, but she held her head high, her eyes slightly hazed and uneasy as fuck.

Dasia slid through the gate but paused a few feet inside as we approached, the gate clanging shut once more behind her.

"Holy fuck," Devil muttered as a brisk breeze ruffled what had at one time been bright red hair.

She hugged herself, her clothing little more than rags stained with blood and who the fuck knew what else.

"Dasia?" I stepped close, unable to touch her shivering body. "The fuck happened to you?"

She glanced beyond me toward the club, fear in her eyes. "Is Miss Pia here?"

"She's inside."

"Who the fuck did this to you?" Devil ground out, and I glanced over to find his entire body vibrating as he ripped off his zipper-down.

*Trouble.*

I pulled my cell from my pocket again.

Dasia warily eyed Devil as he placed his sweatshirt around her.

"Put your arms in," he told her, his tone gentler than I'd expected for the anger tensing him the fuck up. He gently gathered her hair out of the way as she did as told.

"Got a friend here to see you, little lamb," I told my woman when she answered, keeping an eye on Devil while he attempted to set Dasia at ease, "and you better get out here before Devil eats her up."

"Who is it?"

"Dasia."

"*What*?" She fumbled with her phone as I took in Devil's instincts to care for Dasia. He had a good thirteen or so years on the girl—the fucker was in for a crushing eye opener.

The club door slammed open behind me, and I turned as Pia rushed toward us. "Dasia!" she called out with a rush of happiness and fear in her voice.

I clenched my teeth, expecting her hormones to bring on a rush of tears as she'd been doing with anything even remotely tiresome, worrisome, or annoying.

"Holy... Wow." She pulled up short of yanking Dasia into her arms and lowered her head to better see the young woman's pale face. My ever-observant little lamb. "Dasia?"

The young girl broke down and threw herself into Pia's arms. Pia glanced up at me while wrapping Dasia in her embrace, but I shrugged, shaking my head, letting her know I didn't know jack shit.

She glanced at Devil, but he couldn't seem to tear his focus off Dasia's mess of red hair knotted to fucking hell—and the fact more skin showed than was healthy for a young woman in the cool September breeze.

Devil's focus dropped to Dasia's ass barely covered by ripped cotton shorts.

"She's only seventeen," Pia hissed at him.

He didn't twitch.

I elbowed the fucker. "She's seventeen," I growled, "and beat to fucking hell, you sick *fuck*."

Devil blinked—and cursed. "Gotta figure this out, Ryker. Gotta get whoever did this to her and end him."

I knew the feeling—too fucking well.

Tension continued to radiate off Devil as Pia murmured to Dasia, stroking her back through Devil's sweatshirt. "You're safe with us, understand?"

Dasia nodded against Pia's shoulder, a shudder rippling through her. "I-I knew I would be if I found you here."

"How did you know where to look for me?"

"The biker's rockers on his cut—I knew you were dead gone on him, and I'd seen enough lust in a man's eyes to know he wouldn't be able to stay away from you."

Pia glanced up at me, and I recognized the itch she confessed to daily to smooth the furrow between my eyebrows.

"What happened to you, Dasia?" I asked, my voice low, seemingly unthreatening, but Pia's gaze narrowed at me before glancing to Devil and back again.

"*Not* the conversation for right now, Ryker. We need to take her home and get her cleaned up. Warm and fed."

I forced myself to take a calming breath while noting Dasia's bare, hairy legs and old, beat up sneakers. Trust Pia to go straight to the mothering while I craved answers and retribution.

"I'll go get the truck," I muttered, thankful as fuck my woman was my opposite. She knew best, always did. Wrapped around her little finger? Bet your goddamn life.

"Devil," I barked, ripping his focus off Dasia. "Give Vigil a call for me. Let him know what's going on."

A muscle ticked in his jaw, but he nodded, finally tearing himself away to stalk toward the club as I made for my truck around back of the club. "Call me!" he hollered with a glare—he would want to know it all. Every bloody, sick, and gory detail.

Dasia had obviously stabbed him in the goddamn groin—and possibly heart. I expected there would be hell to pay for whoever else had dared to touch her.

Three hours later, Dasia slept in the spare bedroom on Pia's old bed we'd made up in the guest room. Showered, hair brushed out, finally calm—and with a full belly she claimed to not have had in weeks— she passed the fuck out.

I laid on our bed, Pia facing me same as every night, our hands clasped in front of us. "Did she tell you what happened?"

"Not everything, but enough to know it's going to cause trouble for you and your brothers."

I raised an eyebrow and waited. Vigil had texted me once for details I hadn't been able to supply. Devil had hit me up five times—and I'd finally told him to fuck off.

Obsessive fucker.

Pia exhaled a heavy breath. "She escaped a container down at the harbor. There were at least twenty other young girls with her."

*Trouble, indeed.*

I swallowed the need to shed blood that itched across my skin. "Sex slaves."

Pia nodded, studying my face. "That's what I'm afraid of."

"Fuck."

*When Devil finds out...* The sick fuck had a thing for tying women up, controlling them and their pleasure. If he had his heart set on Dasia, he had one hell of a fight ahead of him, and not just finding justice for her.

Pia tightened her hold on my hands. "Promise me you'll talk to the officers about this situation before taking off like a vigilante grim reaper. If you're going to take action, do it with your brothers at your back."

I had too much in my damn head to respond.

"Ryker McGrath, you're going to be a father," Pia said, her tone hardening, her eyes filling with piss and vinegar. "You have to think outside your own desires with this one. Put this kid first. Put me first."

A slow and steady, intentional as fuck exhale emptied my lungs as I tugged her closer, so I could lose myself in the softness of her skin and let the thoughts of what needed to be done to bring justice for Dasia go. "I wouldn't dream of anything else, little lamb."

She raised an eyebrow. "You're sure about that?"
"Yep. I'm a changed man."
She snorted.
"The last thing I'm going to do is put myself in a

place that might take me away from the two best things I've been lucky as fuck to find."

"Language, my badass biker."

"*Kiss* my bad ass, little lamb."

Her smile dimpled her cheek and stole my breath, and at the soft touch of her lips to mine, I pushed aside all thoughts of vengeance.

It could wait.

## THE END

---

# ABOUT THE AUTHOR

Lynn Burke is a full-time mother, voracious gardener, and International Bestselling Author of hot romance books. A country bumpkin turned Bay Stater, she enjoys her chowdah and Dunkin Donuts when not trying to escape the reality of city life.

# ALSO BY LYNN BURKE

Blood Born Series

Bonds of Worship Series

Darkest Desires Series

Dark Leopards MC

Devil's Outlaws MC

Elite Escort Series

Fallen Gliders MC

Found by Fate Series

Midnight Sun Series

Missing Link Series

Risso Family Series

Sandy Ridge Series

Vicious Vipers MC

**Standalone Titles:**

Abel's Obsession

Divulging Secrets

Healing Storms

In Between

The Playboy Bachelor